A Man
Cleansed
by God

Other titles by John E. Beahn
in the TAN Legends Series

A MAN BORN AGAIN
A Novel Based on the Life of Saint Thomas More

A MAN OF GOOD ZEAL
A Novel Based on the Life of Saint Frances de Sales

A RICH YOUNG MAN
A Novel Based on the Life of Saint Anthony of Padua

A Man
Cleansed
by God

A Novel Based on the Life of Saint Patrick

JOHN E. BEAHN

TAN Books
Charlotte, North Carolina

This book was first published in 1959 by The Newman Press in Westminster, Maryland, under the title *A Man Cleansed By God: A Novel Based on St. Patrick's Confession*. The TAN Legends edition has been re-typeset and revised to include corrections of typographical errors and updating of punctuation, spelling and diction.

TAN Legends edition copyright © 2013 TAN Books.

Cover design by Caroline Kiser.

ISBN: 987-0-9575978-8-1

Cataloging-in-Publication data on file with the Library of Congress.

Printed and bound in the United States of America.

TAN Books
Charlotte, North Carolina
www.TANBooks.com
2013

*To these spiritual sons of Saint Patrick
and my friends*

Rt. Rev. Msgr. John J. Daly
Rev. Edward J. A. Nestor (R.I.P.)
Rev. Daniel M. Mcgrath
Rev. William A. Dumps
Rev. Patrick J. Begley

I am the true vine, and my Father is the vine-dresser. Every branch in me that bears no fruit He will take away; and every branch that bears fruit He will cleanse, that it may bear more fruit.

John 15:1–2

PROLOGUE

THE old man pulled his bench forward until he could brace himself with both elbows on the table and look fixedly, even belligerently, at the blank parchment spread before him. He put the stylus to the parchment tentatively and waited stiffly as though the instrument should write of itself. For a long time he waited, but the stylus remained motionless. He lifted it and studied disappointedly the minute black mark imprinted on the writing surface. He placed the stylus into position again, lifted it, then repeated the motion several times before he realized that he was beginning to intrigue himself by his ability to place the point of the stylus precisely on the original mark.

He leaned back on his bench and let his eyes wander as they desired, to the window and the green countryside, sparkling with the wetness of dew in the early morning light. A little distance away, the ground disappeared where it dropped down to form the valley; when it reappeared, far in the distance, it rose steadily until it vanished in the morning mist that shrouded the mountains.

God had fitted him better to cross all of that country, despite his years, than to express in writing the thoughts that crowded his mind and must find their way to the parchment. Reluctantly, he forced his attention to the page, leaned forward deliberately and placed the stylus again on the original black mark.

The stylus moved slowly, arduously. "I am Patrick, a sinner, most unlearned . . ." He lifted the stylus and regarded the characters approvingly. That was what he desired to say! ". . . least of all the faithful, utterly despised by many," he added readily.

Again the stylus stopped. He lifted it and bit the end carefully yet hatefully. Why did it write so slowly for him when it could write so quickly and gracefully for Sechnall? Or why had it written for Sechnall words that had travelled swiftly across all Ireland so that all the Irish heard and memorized the praises of Patrick when they should hear and memorize only the praises of God? Very properly Sechnall had referred to God—"Hear, all ye lovers of God"—but he had veered quickly from the thought of God to thoughts of God's creatures: "Hear, all lovers of God, the holy merits of the man blessed in Christ, Bishop Patrick, who, because of his perfect life, is likened to the angels and deemed equal to the Apostles."

Patrick stabbed the disobedient stylus at the parchment. "Write! Write!" he grumbled. "Answer the man! Tell what must be told of me so that men may forget me and think only of God!"

Slowly, the stylus resumed its work. "I am imperfect in many things and I must, by this work, tell all my brethren and kinsmen in Christ what kind of person I am, despite my little training and education in the art of words. I cannot be silent; I am compelled to tell the great benefits and great graces which the Lord deigned to bestow upon me, even while I suffer and blush at revealing my lack of education.

"There has been disseminated among you a poem written by my friend, Bishop Sechnall, who permitted his affection to becloud his judgment and his stylus to overpower his perception. Would that he had never written it, for it misleads all who hear it by representing me as a man 'constant in the fear of God, steadfast in faith, God's faithful servant, apostolic example and model, humble, untiring, confident in God,' and much more which my guilty ears cannot endure. Would to God I were such; but neither am I nor shall I ever trust myself to be as long as I am in this body of death.

"Strong is he who strives daily to turn me from the faith and from the purity of the true religion to which I have devoted the days of my life; the hostile flesh tugs me toward death, that is, toward the forbidden satisfaction of fleshly desires. And I know that I did not lead a perfect life as did others of the faithful. I acknowledge it before my Lord.

"I must give thanks unceasingly to God Who so often pardoned my folly and my carelessness and so many times spared me from His wrath. He had mercy on me thousands and thousands of times. He cleansed me and made me fit so that I should become what was far from me. . . ."

A Man
Cleansed
by God

1

GOD began the work of cleansing Patrick for his destined mission on a pleasant day in the spring of 401.

On that day the sixteen-year-old Patrick sat atop the wall of the fort at Bannaventa and watched with practiced eyes the recruits who marched and countermarched, wheeled and halted in the parade area below him. Occasionally he grimaced with professional disdain as one or another erred awkwardly, halting the whole company and causing them to begin the maneuver again. He had witnessed the scene often, had seen other recruits begin as awkwardly as these, had watched their progress, had seen them complete their training and depart to take their places as Roman infantrymen—to become a part of that great force on which the peace of the civilized world depended.

Most often he watched the drill master. The man was hard and fit, wearing helmet, armor, sword and shield without effort, despite the warmth of Britain's spring. He held his place in the very center of the parade area, lifting his feet rhythmically in cadence with the recruits, his voice ringing clearly.

Patrick drew up his feet and wrapped his arms around his knees, the better to enjoy the scene. Someday he too would be a hardened veteran of campaigns spanning the earth; someday he would have, as a reward, a post in such

3

a garrison as this at Bannaventa—not as drill master but as a Decurion like his father.

He frowned as a figure appeared from the shade of the buildings on the far side of the parade area. Young Father Alexius, village priest, dispenser of the sacraments to the women who attended Mass, tutor of the officers' children— and of the officers themselves when necessary—censor of soldiers' morality, had come again to complain against him because he, son of the Decurion, would not demean himself to a priest as did the sons of lesser men.

He watched disagreeably as the priest blundered into the class of recruits, disengaged himself and continued to the commandant's quarters. Patrick wondered how many more times his father must ignore this priest and dismiss his complaints before Father Alexius would abandon his efforts. He considered briefly the choice of remaining disin- terestedly where he was or of presenting himself boldly to hear the priest's latest accusation of disrespect. The priest's complaints were the more interesting, he decided.

He leaned forward and looked down. "Move, Coco," he ordered his dog; with lithe ease he lowered himself, held momentarily to the top of the wall with his fingers, and let his body plunge the remaining distance to the ground. He was big beyond his sixteen years, strong beyond his youthfulness, contemptuous of others in the knowledge of his father's position and his own future. Nature had given him the broad, flat bones that presaged a big and power- ful man of the breed that traditionally led the legionnaires. Let weaker, retiring youths devote themselves to the les- sons and prayers fostered by Father Alexius; he was des- tined for greater achievements—perhaps even greater than his father's.

When he pushed into his father's quarters, Father Alexius seemed to have finished his current complaint and was in the act of summarizing all of his charges against Patrick. Decurion Calpornius sat languidly on a bench, leaning back against the wall, obviously uninterested and listening only because army regulations required "courtesy to all priests and bishops of the Holy Roman Church."

Calpornius motioned his son to a seat beside him then interrupted the priest. "You are not a drill master, Father Alexius. You cannot expect to form all those you teach into one mold as do our drill masters."

"A certain order, Decurion, is necessary in society as much as in the military," the priest answered, "and Patrick . . ."

"And Patrick," Calpornius said harshly, "is a freeborn citizen of Rome, son of the Decurion." He stood up indignantly, his heavy body towering above the slight figure of the priest.

The gesture failed to intimidate Father Alexius. Patrick reflected that if courage were the only consideration, he would be this priest's most enthusiastic admirer and friend. "You are excessively indulgent to Patrick, Decurion," the priest answered.

"I know my son," Calpornius said heatedly. "I know him as you do not and do not care to know him."

"I know him," Father Alexius charged, "as a youth of some promise; but I know him now as arrogant, uneducated and disinterested in education, disrespectful to lawful authority, unmindful of his eternal salvation."

"And I know him as one who will be worthy one day to lead Roman legionnaires while they defend you and the whole Christian world against barbarians," Calpornius retorted angrily. "I have spent my life trying to develop such men from soldiers and never succeeded. Then such a man was born to me and you presume to impose your discipline on him." The Decurion wheeled away from the priest and strode angrily to the far end of the room.

"I will give you an opportunity to know the boy," Calpornius resumed. "I have been summoned to headquarters at Deva. While I go there, Patrick will go to our villa. He will be responsible for everything concerning it—care of the house and fields, direction of the guards, servants and field workers. Go with him, even for a week, Father Alexius. See for yourself that the boy knows much that is not learned from books."

Patrick started as he heard his father's proposal. *He* would be in charge of the villa? His father must have devised that at this very moment and for the sole purpose of impressing Father Alexius.

He was inured to his father's extravagant praise. And he was amused that it now seemed to confound Father Alexius as though the priest were unable to understand a father's appreciation of his son. The priest glanced from father to son, patently unable to believe that a father would express his pride so freely in the presence of the son or that the son would not be embarrassed by the fulsome praise of his father.

"You would be most welcome at our villa, Father Alexius," Patrick offered sardonically.

For a moment, the priest studied Patrick soberly as he might some stranger rather than one whom he had known since Decurion Calpornius had assumed command of Bannaventa Hiberna six years before. "I shall be happy to accompany you," he accepted.

*   *   *   *   *

Patrick's assumption of authority at the villa began with unusual difficulties. Departure of the Decurion for distant Deva prompted a tendency to laxness among the servants and guards.

Patrick first noted the new attitude when the guards appointed to duty at the gates neglected to polish their armor. He asked formally and recorded their names, though he knew both, to be reported for disciplinary action by the Decurion. The action discouraged others of the detail from imitating such carelessness.

In subsequent hours, he found it necessary to scold the supervisor of the fields for permitting the workers to idle; then discovered that the house servants were also affected. He stormed about the villa, stirring the household to renewed activity, seemingly oblivious of the priest following him. When they sat down for dinner, however, Patrick was completely self-possessed as his father himself would have been; he exerted himself to entertain the priest with stories of earlier adventures in the area of the villa.

Coco served also as a diversion. Patrick commanded the dog to lie quietly by his bench during the meal but, after dinner, had the dog demonstrate a seemingly endless variety of poses, dances and errands, all of which Coco performed with evident zest.

The priest was quietly amused but became thoughtful also as the demonstration of Coco's prowess continued. "Patrick," he asked after a time, "if Coco will perform so eagerly when you speak single words to him in a soft voice, is it necessary for you to speak so loudly and harshly in order to direct the guards and servants?"

Patrick smiled secretively. "My father taught me that loud noises and threats eliminate the necessity for administering blows or the lash."

"But must you become so angry?"

The question seemed to puzzle Patrick. "I do not become angry," he denied. "We cannot become angry with those who are not our equals," he explained. "The drill master always seems angry when he is training recruits," he elaborated, "but he is not truly angry. Neither am I when I threaten the servants. Father says that fear makes men respond more quickly." He was puzzled that this priest, who seemed to possess all knowledge when he lectured, should be so ignorant concerning the ordinary matters of daily life. Perhaps it was this ignorance of such things that caused or contributed to the difficulties between them.

"Fear," Father Alexius repeated thoughtfully. He nodded his head slowly in agreement. "Fear makes some men obey others; fear makes all men obey God."

Patrick laughed uncomfortably. He did not wish to pursue the subject.

"There is one difference between God and man," the priest continued. "God merely gave us His commandments. He does not shout nor reveal His anger and thus frighten men to obey Him. Perhaps He should; then men would strive more diligently to know Him and His power, and would obey Him more quickly."

Patrick stood up to put an end to the monologue. "I have duties, Father Alexius," he excused himself. He wished to forget as quickly as he could the priest's analogy between God and men.

In the days that followed, the priest did not revive the subject. He seemed content to observe while Patrick established his control over the men of the guard, instituted projects to be performed by the field workers, and supervised the house servants.

Patrick was aware of the priest trailing after him. For a time, he expected some word of interference, under the guise of advice, and was prepared to reject such offers rudely to remind the priest that he was merely a guest and not responsible for the welfare of the villa and its people. He relaxed gradually as the priest neither spoke nor indicated criticism. Patrick began to realize that the enforced companionship was accomplishing something more than that appreciation which his father desired of Father Alexius; he became aware that it was encouraging in him a different attitude toward the priest. When the first week ended, he recognized that a friendship had started which promised to endure and intensify. He considered the prospect with a certain satisfaction.

A shout awakened him on the first night of the second week. Patrick tumbled from his couch, momentarily confused with the heaviness of sleep, and stared at the small, steady flame of the night lamp. A second and third shout awakened him completely—the guard was crying an alarm! Coco barked sharply and stood beside the couch looking alertly toward the doors that opened into the garden.

Patrick threw off his night clothes and dressed hurriedly. The shouted alarm—certainly a warning of attack by humans rather than by animals—was incredible; no human would dare to attack the villa of a decurion of Imperial Rome. Other cries rose up in the night—the shouts of men and screams of terrified women.

He snatched up a short sword and plunged through the doors to the garden, comfortably aware of Coco beside him. He could not see in the dense blackness of the night, but he knew the path to the guards' quarters sufficiently well that he needed no light. On every side, the night was filled with human voices, some crying out in terror, some cursing; he heard voices shouting in a language he did not understand.

At the gateway from the garden, Coco suddenly snarled. Patrick raised his sword to strike some unseen adversary, but powerful hands grasped him. He spun sharply, breaking the hold of the unknown, and lifted his sword again to strike. Coco's snarl, rising suddenly to a gasping bark, distracted him momentarily, then powerful arms and bodies overwhelmed him and bore him helplessly to the ground.

He heard someone speak. The words, in a foreign tongue, were unintelligible, but he could understand them as orders. Those who held him bound his arms quickly behind him. Again the voice of the leader sounded an order, and Patrick heard clearly the word "Neal"—these raiders were Irish, the barbaric subjects of the Irish King Neal. Two of them lifted him roughly to his feet.

Patrick could see slightly; his eyes had become accustomed to the darkness. There were five in the group, but three left immediately on other missions, and the remaining two held his arms and began to urge him toward some destination.

Dimly on the ground, Patrick saw something white. Coco! With sudden madness, he kicked at the legs of the man on his right and lunged against him, knocking the man down, then turned quickly to kick the other. But the barbarian was alert and smashed his fist into Patrick's face, knocking him to the ground. The blow dazed and sickened him. The two lifted him again—the one he had attacked brandished a heavy club and muttered some threat in his own tongue. Patrick stumbled forward in the direction the two urged.

"I was then sixteen years of age," he recorded later in his *Confession.* "I did not know the true God—I did not believe in the living God, nor had I from my childhood. I was taken into captivity to Ireland with many other people and deservedly so, because we turned away from God, and did not obey His commandments, and did not heed our priests when they reminded us of our salvation."

* * * * *

The shouts and cries in the night diminished as the raiders completed their mission. Assured momentarily of their lives, women and children changed their terrified screams to a softer wailing, men changed their belligerent shouts to low rumbling words of comfort.

Vaguely Patrick discerned groups in front of him and his two captors; he sensed that more followed, all converging on some point prearranged by the Irish. He raged inwardly and ineffectually, for he was responsible for the villa and its household; he raged at the effrontery of these invaders who not only dared to penetrate the very heart of Roman Britain but to attack the villa of his father, a Decurion. His rage was the greater because of his helplessness.

The raiders maintained a swift pace despite the darkness, apparently hurrying their human booty before legionnaires could be summoned from the hiberna at Bannaventa or other small forts of the district. Their haste would not save them, Patrick convinced himself. Roman soldiers would pursue and slaughter every member of the band.

The sky lightened until Patrick was able to see the long column of captives ahead of him. Their number astonished him—"many thousands," he estimated. He recognized some—servants, guards, and field workers from the villa—but saw many more he did not recognize who must have been seized from the surrounding countryside. He looked among them vainly for Father Alexius, then attempted to look backward, but both guards, big men who wore on their heads the battle horns of their savage people, seized his arms roughly. Patrick shook their hands free, causing one to laugh admiringly but amusedly. The guard spoke shortly to his fellow and both laughed.

"You had better laugh now," Patrick threatened. "You'll have little to laugh about when the Legion finds us."

His captors looked at him. Unable to understand his words, they seemed to understand his threatening expression and laughed derisively.

The sun's rays lighted a high, dappled sky that gave promise of a clear, spring day, ideal for the legionnaires who would pursue—who, even now, might be hurrying after them. He felt some slight misgivings as he recognized the southwestward direction of their march into a region that had never been friendly to Rome and Roman soldiery. Despite the great benefits they had enjoyed from their conquerors, these people were often suspected of harboring and protecting Irish raiders.

The sun climbed higher. It was directly overhead when the column came to a river where more of the barbarians, guarding a countless number of boats, awaited them. Hopefully, Patrick glanced back the way they had come. He could see only captives and captors and quiet British countryside. The Legion had been unable to form pursuing

units to intercept the raiders while still on British soil—
perhaps they had not been informed of the raid for many
hours after it happened; but the Legion would follow. They
would encounter greater difficulty pursuing to Ireland but,
whatever the cost and however great the difficulty, Rome's
legions would avenge this insult and reclaim her citizens
and subjects.

"Hoping, Patrick?"

Patrick spun around, his spirits lifting at the familiar
sound of Father Alexius' voice. He checked the glad words
of recognition at discovery of one from whom he could
draw strength; the priest was not looking at him. Father
Alexius was searching, as Patrick had done, the path they
had travelled, but his expression was mournful and without hope. The priest himself needed encouragement. "The
legionnaires will follow," Patrick said confidently. He must
give encouragement, not ask it. He must demonstrate again
that he was the youth his father claimed him to be.

Their captors pushed them into a boat with six others.
Patrick recognized a guard from the villa and a field worker,
both of them fatigued and dispirited; the other four were
similarly crushed, for all of them slumped down despon-
dently, sitting against the side of the boat. With elaborate
unconcern, Patrick remained standing, watching the boats
glide away from the bank, like one who waited patiently
the certain arrival of those who would release them in
good time.

*   *   *   *   *

It was an effort to maintain his attitude during the
two days and nights that the boats moved irregularly,

tacking first to the north, then to the south against winds more favorable for leaving Ireland than approaching it. He attempted to arouse the others from their despondent lethargy by speaking of the preparations of the soldiers who would most certainly follow them; none was sufficiently encouraged to raise his head. He felt himself affected by their hopelessness and abandoned the effort to help them.

On the third day a shout from far in the distance carried over the water. Patrick stood and looked ahead curiously. The shout must have signalled a sighting of Ireland, but he could see nothing other than the great multitude of boats bobbing with the motion of the waves and, beyond them, the stretches of open sea. Far ahead, a green mist seemed to rise from the water. Ireland? If that green mist were in fact Ireland, it seemed as unreal as his own situation. He watched, and the mist did indeed materialize until it became green pasture land and darker green forests. The armada converged onto a point of the coast where a river, the Boyne, spilled into the sea.

Another wearying, though more leisurely overland, march began. In their own homeland and apparently confident they were safe from pursuit, the Irish raiders permitted their captives to walk slowly. They came to villages of varying sizes, but all of them nestling at the bottom of low hills, each dominated by a kind of wall made of bare poles set upright in the ground to enclose the residence and other buildings of the local lord.

Men, women and children came from the houses to stare, to wave gayly at King Neal's men and to shout taunts at the captives. On each such occasion Patrick straightened and held his head high that these barbarians might see the spirit of a Roman citizen. Beside him, Father Alexius also raised his head. Patrick saw a few others who remembered their proud heritage but fumed that they were so few.

In the late afternoon, they arrived at their destination—a larger village at the foot of a hill on top of which was a very large fort. "Tara," rippled along the column of captives, "the residence of Ireland's King Neal." The prisoners toiled up the hill and through gates into a small enclosure, joined by another set of gates at the opposite end to the larger enclosure. Straw piled high in one corner and scattered about the ground indicated that it was used more frequently for confinement of animals. The captives rushed upon the straw to gather great bundles and spread it on the ground.

They had little time to rest. Men set wine casks and wooden pails of food—a kind of porridge—inside the gates of the enclosure, leaving the captives to scoop it out with their hands. Immediately after, a series of loud shouts announced arrival of a group surrounding a short but powerful man who wore a golden circlet on his head. A lackey shouted loudly in Latin, "Uncover your heads!"

Automatically, Patrick raised his hand to obey the command, surprised that any on this savage island could speak his own tongue. He hesitated briefly, then let his hand fall to his side while his cap remained on his head. If the individual wearing the golden circlet were Ireland's King Neal, he would see that a Roman citizen did not uncover his head to him.

"Uncover your head!" the lackey shouted a second time, looking directly at Patrick.

"Take off your cap, Patrick," Father Alexius urged. "It means nothing."

Patrick held his hands stiffly to his sides. "It means uncovering to a king of barbarians," he answered. "That lackey who speaks Latin is probably a renegade or criminal wherever he lived in the civilized world."

King Neal moved forward among the captives, obviously selecting some for his own fields and household. The Latin-speaking lackey, with another, left the group and walked rapidly toward Patrick and the priest.

Patrick glared disdainfully at the two. "I am a Roman citizen," he began as they neared. The lackey leaped forward without speaking and struck the side of his face a powerful blow. Patrick staggered. His cap fell to the ground.

"Stand with your head uncovered," the lackey growled. He kicked the cap behind him, then waited alertly with his companion for Patrick to move toward it.

"Don't move, Patrick," Father Alexius pleaded beside him. He grasped Patrick's arm and restrained him from lunging forward. "You're tired."

Patrick stood sullenly. King Neal with his retinue stopped briefly to examine the two, appraising them from head to feet. He grunted something in his own tongue, then moved away without indication of interest. Patrick watched malevolently as the group disappeared through the gates leading into the fort.

Father Alexius dropped down wearily on the straw they had gathered for themselves. "That was foolhardy," he said resignedly. "You won't help yourself or any of us by defying these people."

Patrick stepped forward and retrieved his cap. He slapped it viciously against his leg before replacing it on his head. "When the Legion comes, I'll do more than defy them with words."

"Until the Legion comes," Father Alexius retorted, "you might have worked for the King. Perhaps I might also. Working in King Neal's household should be more pleasant than in any other."

"And escape more difficult," Patrick answered. He motioned toward the bare, upright poles forming the wall of the enclosure. "The other lords of Ireland will not have walls as high as their King's," he muttered.

The priest looked across the darkening enclosure crowded with captives. His eyes moved upward on the wall and higher until he looked at the sky, still bright with the afternoon sun. "I can't escape, Patrick," he said regretfully.

Patrick jerked about to confront the priest, indignant that he had abandoned hope and had surrendered to circumstances. "You're more tired than I am," he charged scathingly. "You're already defeated—beaten!"

Father Alexius moved his head in denial. "I'm a priest, Patrick." He nodded generally toward the other captives. "I am probably the only priest among all these people. As long as I am here, these people can receive absolution and Holy Communion." He paused slightly. "As long as I am here, these people can continue to receive the grace of God through the holy sacraments. They need that grace now even more than when they were free."

"Freedom would be more welcome to them," Patrick said bitterly.

"So much the more reason why I must stay," Father Alexius agreed. "God willed all of us to be made captives. God willed me to be here to help others submit to His holy will."

"I won't submit to that," Patrick said sharply.

"What of these others?"

Patrick glanced at the others in the enclosure. Many were women and children—even very small children—who could not escape. And there were men who were husbands of the women and fathers of the children who would not— or should not—attempt to escape. "The Legion will rescue them," he answered.

"If God wills," Father Alexius amended.

"I will escape," Patrick said fiercely.

The priest did not answer immediately. His very silence seemed to echo his words, "If God wills." "You may scale these walls," he agreed, "or similar walls. But you had better plan beyond that moment because you will not have escaped from Ireland merely by scaling the wall of some Irish lord."

"I will make my way to the seacoast and find a boat," Patrick said confidently.

The priest shook his head doubtfully. "You may; or you may be recaptured by some of the Irish. I don't know their laws or customs but I suspect that a reward is paid for recapturing any who escape. Even without a reward, these Irish would be glad to recapture an escaped Britain or Roman. They hate us, Patrick. They've hated us for generations because they've expected invasion by the legions stationed in Britain."

"I am not a Briton," Patrick objected.

The priest raised himself reluctantly. "Think well before you act, Patrick. I am going among the others that they may confess and receive absolution. If someone among them has a pinch of flour, I will celebrate Mass; if someone has more than a pinch, I will be able to give them Holy Communion."

2

PATRICK watched absently as the priest began his work. He saw the sudden stir among the captives as they learned that a priest was among them; even men pushed with the women and children to the corner of the enclosure where Father Alexius stationed himself. He lay back disinterestedly to gaze up at the darkening sky and to plan.

Slavery!

His mind seethed with the hideous reality. He—all of them—were penned together in this enclosure where animals had been penned before them—as though they were mere animals themselves. Unbidden, the image of Coco emerged in his mind, sitting stiffly upright on his hind legs, clearly enjoying the pleasure he gave his master, happy in his role of entertainer. Patrick stifled a groan at the inescapable thought that he must serve others as his dog had served him.

His mind turned restlessly from past to future, re-examining what had happened, contemplating what was about to happen. Occasionally he was aware of the others moving toward or away from Father Alexius. At times, other sounds interrupted him—a woman's sob, a child's complaint, a man's soothing murmur; they firmed rather than distracted him.

He was a captive, marked for sale like some of the Irish themselves who were sold in secret market places in Deva. He had never seen them sold—the priests had succeeded in making such sales illegal and forcing buyers and sellers to meet in secret. But his father had told him of some sales he had attended, and he had been fascinated by the drama of men bidding, one against another, until the auctioneer could not coax or wheedle another bid. He had barely thought of the slaves themselves because they would have been an uninteresting, depressed and dejected lot. When he did think of them, it was merely to agree with those who observed pityingly the good fortune of those pagan Irish who had been transported from among their barbarous fellows into the culture of civilized Rome.

He would not be a slave, he vowed. He who was a free citizen of Rome—and that not by purchase but by the flesh—would preserve that sacred freedom by some means.

He did not sleep. His body was tense with expectancy. He should not have waited until he was confined, he realized. He should have darted from the captors as soon as he had set foot on this accursed island; or he should have run from the column as it toiled from the place of landing to this place of Tara. But those opportunities had passed; he must anticipate the future. There might be a new opportunity when the captives were marched from the enclosure—an excellent opportunity if they were marched out through the same gates by which they had entered.

He tried to anticipate how the captives would issue from the enclosure; his opportunity would be improved if they were permitted to walk in as disorderly a manner as before. He must be alert to every opportunity.

A general movement among the captives attracted his attention. Father Alexius had finished his first work and seemed to have found the flour and wine be needed for the Mass. Patrick raised himself from the straw and moved cautiously across the darkened enclosure until he came to the edge of the crowd and could hear the priest's voice. For a moment he wondered at Father Alexius, who had stated so definitely that he must remain a captive for the benefit of these others; but the first tinge of light above the top of the palisade diverted his attention to his own plans.

*   *   *   *   *

With the fullness of dawn, attendants pushed through the gates with more porridge and indicated that the captives must eat quickly. "The slave market opens early in Ireland," Patrick heard one man say bitterly. He looked quickly to him, alert to enlist some other as eager as himself to escape; but two children, huddled close to the man, would force him to be content with his bitterness.

The attendants reappeared and Patrick watched alertly, hopeful that they would direct the captives through the gates that opened upon the slope above the village; but the two made their way across the enclosure toward the gates opening into the fort. The men shouted in their strange tongue to unseen others who swung open the gates. The prisoners moved forward docilely.

"We had better say goodbye, Patrick."

Patrick turned guiltily to the priest. He had been so intent upon his plans that he had forgotten the other. He clasped Father Alexius' hand without speaking. They walked together toward the fort.

Beyond the open gates, Patrick saw a broad plateau dominated by a great residence; the building was formed of upright poles like the walls of the enclosure, but with the spaces between them sealed with a kind of clay. That would be King Neal's residence. Around it were smaller shelters, similarly constructed. To the left and slightly lower, where the ground sloped somewhat, was an extremely long hall. Midway along this hall was a platform surrounded by a dense throng of Irish, laughing and talking together as at some festival.

Patrick's resentful anger mounted swiftly at the prospect before him—the humiliation of standing on a platform before these barbarous people while they appraised his strength and stature and carriage, then offered a price for him as though he were cattle or oxen.

The first group of the captives—a man, woman, and three children—was hurried to the platform, Apparently this was a family offered for sale as a unit.

The offering clearly displeased one potential buyer, a heavily muscled young man whose thinning red hair rose and fell and tossed about as he moved his head in tempo with his objections. He shouted loudly at the auctioneer and gestured emphatically toward the captive man, demanding that he be permitted to bid for that one member of the group.

To the vast amusement of the crowd, the auctioneer walked aggressively to the edge of the platform and shouted down on the troublesome bidder with equal loudness, effectively ending his complaints. The crowd added their own jeers, apparently demanding that the auction begin.

The sale proceeded rapidly, new captives mounting to the platform even as those sold descended. Patrick saw and ignored the gesture of a guard that he move to the platform.

A guard behind him pushed him roughly and Patrick turned about and struck quick blows on the astonished man. The spectators shouted gleefully at the melee that ended abruptly as other guards rushed upon Patrick and hurried him to the platform.

He looked down at the faces watching him amusedly. "Death to any who buys a Roman citizen as slave!" he shouted. Few understood his words but all could suspect his meaning. They laughed and shouted taunts at him in their own tongue. Patrick raised his clenched fist threateningly, stirring the crowd to louder taunts. He glanced at those immediately in front of the platform who had bid most actively for those who had preceded him. All of them seemed disinterested in him, as though unwilling to buy a youth who promised to produce more of trouble than of value.

The auctioneer walked to the edge of the platform and spoke to the bidders, urging one or another. He gestured toward Patrick, contrasting his age with his physique. The coarse, red-headed bidder spoke once, the others persisted in their silence. Two men, armed with short swords fastened in their belts, leaped to the platform, grasped Patrick, and conducted him through the noisy throng to a small hut. Four men, seated on the ground around the sides of the hut, looked up at him listlessly. One of the guards pointed for Patrick to sit also.

A muted roar from the crowd marked conclusion of another sale. The two attendants who had escorted Patrick again appeared at the entrance to the hut with Father Alexius between them. Patrick started to rise, happy that they were not to be separated, but the priest averted his eyes quickly, indicating that neither should reveal acquaintance with the other.

They had not long to wait. Immediately after Father Alexius, the red-headed bidder appeared at the hut with another attendant, a brutal, heavy-faced man.

"I am Dann," the attendant announced coldly and impersonally in Latin. "Your owner is Master Miliucc, lord of the land of Slemish in the north. If you do your work without causing trouble—" he glanced meaningly at Patrick "—you will be well treated. Any who are lazy or troublesome will be whipped." He continued in a droning voice with a series of regulations Master Miliucc applied to his slaves. "While on the journey to Slemish," he concluded, "you will talk among yourselves only during the morning and evening meals. You will not whisper. You will talk so that I can hear you." Dann turned toward the door of the hut and motioned for the six to follow him.

The crowd greeted the appearance of Patrick raucously, jeering loudly as Master Miliucc, obviously enjoying the disturbance, led a way for the six slaves followed by Dann and another attendant. Patrick glared challengingly at those nearest him, but a shout from Dann reclaimed his attention to the task of following Master Miliucc to the gate.

Patrick drew a deep breath. He was relieved to be free of the mob and of the enclosure. He glanced out over the countryside, peaceful in the early morning sunlight. The downward slope to the village and the country nearby was a misty green but, as the distance increased, the land disappeared into the thicker mist. Below and to the right was the edge of a forest that stretched southward an indeterminate distance.

Impulsively Patrick leaped from the group and ran with long, leaping strides down the steep side of the slope toward the forest. He heard Dann shout after him, then other voices,

probably Master Miliucc's and the other attendant's or even
the other prisoners', startled and enlivened by his escape.

Free! He ran daringly, slipping on the grass wet with
the dew of morning, twisting to regain his balance, running desperately. He measured the shouts of his pursuers
and knew he was increasing his advantage. He saw men
in the village to his left begin running towards him; but he
would be safely in the forest before they could intercept
him. On the level ground at the foot of the slope, he ran
more swiftly, leaped a small brook that would slow some of
his pursuers, and drew near to the protecting trees.

Two woodsmen, drawn by the shouting, stepped suddenly from the trees before him. Patrick changed his
course to avoid them but both, understanding the incident
immediately, shouted at him and raised their wood-axes
threateningly.

He was too close to them to escape their skilled arms;
either of them or perhaps both would have struck the mark.
He halted abruptly, conquered a sudden and unexpected
desire to sink down defeated on the earth, then turned to
face his pursuers.

Dann struck him a savage blow, knocking him down,
then stood over him, cursing in his barbaric native tongue
as though he saw the attempted escape as a personal affront.
The woodsmen and those of the village gathered into a circle, laughing and talking with the excitement of the chase,
until Master Miliucc and the remaining attendant arrived
with the other five captives.

Master Miliucc spoke roughly to Dann and Dann
demanded, "Get up!"

Patrick arose unsteadily in front of his owner, Master
Miliucc. Another stunning blow felled him.

When he opened his eyes again, Patrick was not on the grass where he had fallen, and the sun was much higher than it had been. His body pained. He realized that he had been struck many more blows—probably kicked—after he had fallen unconscious. He was sitting now against the wall of a house in the village, supported from falling by two other slaves beside him.

Instinctively he started to rise, then saw the iron bands about his wrists, joined with a chain that bound him to similar bands on the wrists of the men beside him. He looked along the line of men; all were manacled. At the extreme end was Father Alexius. Dann had been waiting for him to recover consciousness. He approached and stood over Patrick, savagely pleased and looking at him evilly. "Only the journey saved you from the lash," he warned. "We wanted to leave you strength to walk."

Patrick had neither strength nor spirit to reply. His eyes lowered to the manacles and chains that bound him to the others and all of them together. He knew he should regret the penalty he had brought upon the others; yet it was a small penalty, and he knew a gladness that he had made the attempt. The mere attempt was defiance—the mere attempt had preserved his status as a free citizen of Rome. A man must have confidence in something. He would have confidence in himself.

*   *   *   *   *

Patrick stumbled through the journey of the first day, without interest in the country through which they passed and with little consciousness of time. On the second day, the pain of the kicks and blows lessened, and he was able to straighten his body and walk more easily. On the third day, youthful resilience surmounted the remaining bruises, and he became more interested in the country and in his surroundings.

He felt the hostility of the others—not only that of the attendants, but of the others chained together because of his attempted flight. During the morning and evening meals, when they were permitted to talk, none spoke to him. The discovery did not disturb him: He felt far apart from them in the knowledge that they lacked the spirit to do what he had and what he would do again.

On the fifth day they crossed a river which was the southern boundary of Master Miliucc's estates, the land of Slemish. It was a beautiful country of rolling green pastures and darker green woods, of gentle hills and abrupt mountains, of lakes and streams, of herds of cattle and flocks of sheep, of rich fields where men and women ceased their work to look curiously at Master Miliucc, his six new slaves chained together, and the two attendants. It was a beautiful country, Patrick acknowledged, but it was also a prison.

Soon after noon of the sixth day, they came to the village where lived the freemen-artisans who served Master Miliucc. None appeared in the doorways of the houses to shout welcomes or taunts as people of other villages had done; two men working at a forge paused only long enough to glance at the group passing by; the driver of an ox-drawn cart cracked a long whip over the heads of his team, drove them to the side of the road, removed his hat, and stood motionless until Master Miliucc had passed. Patrick's hopes stirred as he saw the signs of fear; these artisans and their families were Master Miliucc's servants, but not his friends.

The lord of Slemish led the way up a hill to his household establishment. It was like all other homes in this barbaric country—the flattened top of a hill rimmed with poles, skinned of their bark and set upright in the ground as a kind of fortification. Two great gates swung open then closed again when the company filed into the enclosure. Within this enclosure was the lord's home, also of poles and white clay—these people had never learned the use of stone and tile and marble as had the civilized peoples subject to Rome. Spaced around the home were smaller buildings—barns, stables, storage houses, quarters for household servants and the like—all constructed of the stripped poles and clay.

Those working within the enclosure stopped only momentarily from their labors. The one sign of human-ness was the appearance of two small girls who ran from the lord's house to welcome Master Miliucc noisily and be lifted in his arms.

Dann assumed his master's position, directed the group into place, then produced a small tool for removing the manacles which bound the slaves together. When he came to Patrick, he paused deliberately as though considering whether or not to release his bands. "You will be watched, boy," he threatened. Roughly he removed the iron bands, moved on to the others, then took a place before them.

"Each of you will be asked his work. If you want to be treated well, you will tell your skills and will use them."

Patrick's attention wandered to the great gates swing-ing open once again to admit a group of men carrying heavy loads of wood, then closing after them. He heard Dann's voice rumbling but did not attend to his words. Again the great gates swung open to admit the ox-drawn cart they had passed on the road. But the gates did not close again as before; the gateman moved away to some other task, letting the gates remain open while another cart trundled from behind a building and moved slowly across the open area toward the gate.

Patrick tensed. He might never again have such an opportunity. As well as he could, without turning his head, he measured his own distance from the gate, and the distance of the cart from the gate. He glanced at Dann and saw that the overseer was preoccupied with the labor of his instructions to the group.

The cart lumbered closer to the gate. Patrick felt himself weaken suddenly as the thought of failure intruded. He expelled the thought and held himself ready, watching the cart's slow progress. He saw the driver flick his long whip over the heads of the animals, turning them.

Patrick leaped from his place and ran desperately. His heart lifted as he saw the perfection of timing—he would be at the gate just in front of the beasts' muzzles, then the cart would block the gateway to his pursuers.

Dann shouted after him—a startled and angry shout. Others shouted. Master Miliucc's voice roared above all the others. Patrick saw the gatemen leap to intercept him, but they were too late. The driver of the cart turned about, startled by the shouting and the sight of Patrick already at the rear of his vehicle.

Patrick lunged forward to dash through the small space before the oxen. He felt, rather than saw, the driver flick his whip downward and tried to leap above the curling lash. He felt the snare coil about his legs, then fell headlong, his legs bound tightly together. Despair overwhelmed him and he had not the spirit to fight against the gatemen when they grasped him.

Master Miliucc's face was red with anger. He roared and seemed to curse in his own strange tongue, urging the gatemen, Dann, and others who ran to help, toward some action. He walked about furiously with his hand upraised and fingers spread, indicating five of something.

Two of the group seized Patrick from the restraining hands of the gatemen, hurried him to the door of a stable and tied him, his face toward the door and his hands stretched above his head. The position revealed the penalty to be exacted and Patrick drew his muscles together expectantly. Instantly the lash scored his back and Patrick's body leaped convulsively. He pressed his lips firmly together and clamped his teeth that no sound might escape. The lash whistled and stung again and again until the prescribed five were counted. Someone—he could not see who—untied the ropes that bound him. His arms dropped to his sides. He succeeded in standing upright for a moment. Then consciousness left him.

3

HE was lying face down in a rack of straw when he opened his eyes again. His back burned as if on fire. He dared not move lest that increase the stinging pain. A horse was in a stall opposite his resting place and he heard more of the animals stamping in stalls beyond his view; he realized that he had been moved from the door of the stable where he had collapsed into the interior. He heard another movement; he could not raise himself nor turn his head, but sensed that a human was in the stable with him. He called weakly, then closed his eyes against the intensity of the pain.

"Sleep if you can," a man's voice murmured with a sympathy that was strangely impersonal. "I'll try to get something later to relieve the pain."

The stable was dark with an impenetrable darkness when he awakened again. His back felt soothed. He moved slightly and felt the sting of the stripes but none of the fire that had tortured him earlier. The unknown must have found something to relieve the pain. He moved more, then struggled up to sit on the side of the rack. In the darkness, he heard another also move.

"Stay where you are!" It was the same voice that had spoken earlier. The man stumbled through the darkness until his searching hand found Patrick's. "Eat this. I have bread for you also."

Obediently Patrick ate what was given him. It tasted of honey and grain. While he ate the bread, the other brought water, then ordered him to lie down again and sleep.

He awakened to the light of dawn that poured into the stable in the form of great square shafts from openings in the wall. His first sight was of a young man rising with apparent reluctance from a pile of straw; he was one of the group that had been chained together on the march from Tara to Slemish. Patrick pushed himself up; he could move again with some ease. The other—Patrick had an impression of an extremely handsome youth of about twenty-two—moved quickly to help, but Patrick needed no assistance.

"You're feeling better?"

Patrick smiled weakly. "Thanks to you, I suppose." He wanted to express or indicate his gratitude to his slender, graceful benefactor, but the young man seemed uninterested in his gratitude or even in him as a person. His manner displayed the same impersonal attitude that had tinged his voice. "I am Patrick," he offered.

The young man acknowledged the information with the briefest movement of his eyes. He stooped and produced two honey cakes with bread and water; from another place he took an earthen bowl. "Turn about," he ordered. "While you eat, I'll put more grease on your back."

Patrick started to turn, but he glimpsed the other's wrist and saw the raw wound where the manacle had chafed the skin. He understood why this young man, with the others, had been so hostile to him during the six days that the manacles had galled their flesh. He felt a sudden repentance that he had caused the wounds on this young man who repaid him by helping him, but he could not properly phrase an apology. He turned his back as the other had ordered. "I am the son of a Roman decurion, Calpornius," he said, as though to explain the inner spirit that had incited him to attempt escape.

The other said nothing. He seemed absorbed in his task of smearing the soothing grease on Patrick's back.

"Who are you?" Patrick asked.

"Victoricus," the other answered simply, "courier from Rome and probationary officer."

Patrick felt abashed as he realized the significance of the answer. Victoricus was not merely a citizen of Rome or son of a decurion; he was actually a Roman and probably of a distinguished Roman family, for it was from among those patricians that the government drew youths for employment as couriers and eventual training as officers. He had offered his own lineage as the reason for attempting what this other, of much more impressive lineage, had not attempted. "I'm very grateful to you," he mumbled awkwardly.

Victoricus finished the task and stepped back. "I'll be more willing to believe that if you do not attempt any more foolhardy escapes."

Patrick eased himself around to face Victoricus. His gratitude dissipated at the unwarranted demand. He certainly would not admit that his attempts had been foolhardy; neither would he promise that he would not repeat them. Mere chafing of the wrists did not justify the other in presenting such a demand.

His strength returned in succeeding days as his wounds healed. He walked more and more frequently to the door of the stable and looked out on the enclosure, looking for Father Alexius. Victoricus applied more grease to his wounds and brought him food—most often a wooden bowl of thick gruel made of oats and meat. "Will they give us more bread," he asked on the fourth day, "or more honey cakes?"

Victoricus' expression was a mixture of amusement and cynicism. "We get gruel and meat, Patrick. Bread and honey cakes—even grease—are the exclusive prerogatives of our Master Miliucc and his little girls." He shrugged his shoulders. "Perhaps he gives bread and cakes also to Dann and his other faithful lackeys."

Patrick considered the information briefly. "You brought bread and honey cakes. You found grease to put on my back." He looked wonderingly at Victoricus. "You went into Master Miliucc's house and took them," he analyzed.

Victoricus did not answer. He took a long-handled, forked tool from its place against the wall, plunged it into a pile of fodder and tried to swing the tangled mass toward a feed rack. His uneven movements loosened the burden and it fell to the floor. Patrick saw the evidences of inexperience. He was rapidly learning more of his companion. He wondered at the man who could not perform a simple task, but who could boldly invade the house of Master Miliucc when necessary to assist another; yet at the same time resent another's efforts to escape. "What would the penalty have been if you were discovered?"

Victoricus had knelt to gather the scattered forage together. He shook his head slightly as though wondering himself what penalty might have been exacted, then resumed his work.

"You took a greater risk by entering Master Miliucc's house than you would by attempting to escape," Patrick persisted.

Victoricus looked up slowly. His expression was grave. "Patrick, the word escape comes quickly to your lips. I hoped you had learned your folly." He stood up. "You and I have been assigned to care for this stable and the horses in it. But I have a separate responsibility—to prevent you from escaping."

Patrick regarded Victoricus incredulously. "You wouldn't prevent me?"

Victoricus smiled grimly. "I have the choice of preventing you or of receiving ten lashes. Which would you choose?"

Patrick tried to revive his firmness of spirit; but he knew that the beating he had received when he first attempted to escape, the whipping after his second attempt here at Slemish, and the knowledge of Victoricus' care of him—even entering Master Miliucc's house—had weakened his will. "You do not intend to remain here as a slave?"

Victoricus shook his head. "But I will look to God for the opportunity to escape, and He may not give it to me for a long time."

Patrick's resentment stirred feebly. "You should have asked God to prevent them from bringing you here," he said bitterly.

"He has protected me from doing something so foolish as to deserve the lash," Victoricus answered sharply. "When it was necessary for me to endanger myself—by entering Miliucc's house for that grease and food in the middle of the night—God safeguarded me because I did what was necessary and not something foolish. I had to walk past Miliucc's sleeping cubicle, past the sleeping cubicles of Dann and the household guards, past the sleeping cubicles of two servants, in order to take the grease for your back and food to give you strength. Who but God prevented one or another or all of them from discovering me and killing me immediately?" He drew a deep, indignant breath. "You don't know God, do you, Patrick?"

The question startled Patrick. It seemed almost an echo
of Father Alexius' thought about the fear God might use
to make men strive more diligently to know Him and His
power, and to obey Him more readily. "I know God," he
defended himself. "But I don't believe we should wait for
Him to lead us by the hand any more than we should expect
Him to send angels to help us clean this stable."

Victoricus studied him hesitantly. "Could a priest persuade you of God's providence?" he asked with elaborate
casualness.

Patrick smiled at the other's efforts to ensnare him
while concealing the presence of a priest at Master Miliucc's establishment. "Father Alexius and I are old friends,"
he retorted. He enjoyed the astonishment of Victoricus.
"I've tried to see him from the doorway," he explained
regretfully. "Where is he?"

Victoricus was more subdued. "He works for the
miller." He looked hopefully at Patrick. "He will be here
tonight. One man has obtained wine, and Father Alexius
has gathered enough flour for Mass and Holy Communion."

*   *   *   *   *

Despite the warmth of Father Alexius' greeting when
he embraced Patrick in the dark stable, Patrick felt ill at
ease and as a stranger to the other slaves, both men and
women, who devised to steal into the stable that night to
attend Mass and receive Holy Communion. He became
more conscious of his estrangement from them when Father
Alexius assigned him to stand by the door to warn if anyone
approached, as though the priest, knowing his attitude, dismissed him from participating in the service.

A loneliness afflicted Patrick. He watched carefully for any movement outside the stable, but he was aware of the priest's voice and the muted responses of the group, begging God to release them. He could understand the helplessness that led the women to pray and even the lack of spirit characteristic of most of the men; he could not understand Father Alexius nor Victoricus, for he knew the courage of both. He looked at the top of the palisade, outlined faintly against the sky. He would solve this problem of release, not by prayer, but by surmounting that palisade.

The Mass ended. Cautiously Patrick prevented the group from leaving together; he released them through the door one by one at intervals so that their footfalls would not combine into sufficient sound to cause an alarm. Father Alexius, last of the company, stopped near the door and drew Patrick farther in with Victoricus.

"Four men escaped tonight," the priest said quietly. "We can pray that they are successful and reach Britain." He slipped away quietly.

Patrick let his hopes surge without restraint. "If they reach Britain," he said in hushed but excited tones, "the Legion will know exactly where we are." He waited, but Victoricus did not answer. Patrick heard him moving toward his pile of straw; he stumbled after him. "Victoricus! If the Legion knows where we are, they can rescue us by raiding instead of by invasion." The other continued his silence. "You seem to doubt they will come," Patrick charged disagreeably.

"Patrick," the Roman answered softly, "four of us were dispatched from Rome at intervals of one week. Each of us was sent to the commander of the Twentieth Legion at Deva. Each of us carried the same order that the Legion

withdraw from Britain and return to Rome with the greatest possible speed. I was on the way to Deva when I was
captured by these Irish."

"That can't be," Patrick protested.

Victoricus was not interested in convincing Patrick that
his information was correct.

"Rome has already recalled the other two legions
assigned to Britain," Patrick persisted. "If the Twentieth
withdraws, Britain will be defenseless. The Irish, the Picts—
barbarians can sweep into the country from any direction."

"Barbarians *can* invade Britain," Victoricus agreed.
"That is a future possibility. The present actuality is that
barbarians have already invaded France—all the tribes of
the north seem to be moving. So Rome is assigning the
legions to those places where invasion is already happen-
ing, even though it should expose other areas of the Empire
to possible invasion. Rome itself is threatened."

"But you didn't deliver the message," Patrick countered hopefully. "The commander . . ."

"Patrick, I was the third courier. On my way I learned
that the courier who preceded me was captured in France by
German barbarians; but when I arrived in Britain, I learned
that the first courier had succeeded in his mission and was
already at Deva. Since there was no more need for haste, I
waited for the courier following me so that we could enjoy
ourselves along the way. We had progressed only as far
as the country around Bannaventa when I could have been
at Deva." He paused regretfully. "That is how it happened
that I was captured by these raiders."

Patrick slumped dejectedly onto the pile of straw
that was his bed. He felt a fearful wonderment as though
the world were suddenly disintegrating. The Empire

threatened? actually attacked and invaded? legions overwhelmed and driven back by barbarians? the great Imperial City threatened? "I don't—," he began, then suddenly
changed his words to make them more truthful. "I won't
believe you," he said firmly.

He knew he did believe Victoricus. He believed despite
the desire of his heart to disbelieve. The order from Rome
explained the order for his father to report to Deva—the
order which his father had used as excuse for sending him
from the hiberna to the villa with Father Alexius.

He lay back on the straw, staring into the black void,
strangely impressed by the unrelated series of events that
had brought him to his status as a slave of Master Miliucc.
He remembered Father Alexius' repugnant words, "God
willed all of us to be made captives."

God willed that he be a captive? a slave? He would
not believe that! It was nothing more than another of the
priest's fanciful thoughts. Patrick moved about restlessly to
drive the dread possibility from his mind.

His mind would not release the thought but held to it
tenaciously. He remembered his race toward freedom, his
flight down the slope of Tara—the elation he had felt in the
certainty of his freedom—and the inexplicable appearance
of the two woodsmen who had defeated him in the very
moment of success. He remembered the moment here at
Master Miliucc's when one more step would have assured
his freedom—but that step had been thwarted by the astonishing skill of an ox-cart driver. "God willed all of us to be
made captives."

"I won't submit to that," he had told Father Alexius. He
would not! The four who had escaped this very night had
not submitted. Neither would he. He would devise means,

as they had, for scaling the palisade, finding his way to the sea and a boat that would return him to Britain. He scowled into the darkness. Let that be God's will!

He fought to fix the resolution firmly in his mind and heart. The son of a Roman decurion could not submit placidly to misfortune, could not disguise cowardice or mere lack of spirit by describing it as submission to God's will.

Suppose he failed to escape?

He thrust the thought instantly from his mind. He would not fail.

But suppose he did fail? Suppose God had indeed willed him to be a captive?

He tossed about restlessly, distracting himself from the doubt that persisted despite his efforts to eject it.

The invincible Empire had been invaded, the unconquerable legions conquered. Who, other than God, could have devised means for shattering the two certainties of earthly life? Only God could have willed that.

He raised himself and sat up. Deliberately he forced himself to listen to the hushed movements of the horses in their stalls; but they were captives—by the will of God—and their movements reminded him the more forcefully of his own captivity. He lay down again to stare into the darkness.

He was without power to resist the thoughts that surged into his mind or to stop the flow of memory. "God merely gave us His commandments," he heard Father Alexius again. "He does not shout nor reveal His anger and thus frighten men to obey Him. Perhaps He should; then men would strive more diligently to know Him and His power, and would obey more readily." A dread fastened upon Patrick: Perhaps God had shouted and revealed His anger.

Father Alexius had also said, "God willed all of us to be made captives." The voice of Victoricus followed immediately, "I will look to God for the opportunity to escape and He may not give it to me for a long time."

The blackness of the stable transformed suddenly into an embodiment of his own future—dark and impenetrable. The years extended indefinitely into the abyss of nothingness—how long? how long? Terror possessed him. He raised himself again from the straw, swung his feet from the rack to the floor, and stole quietly to the door.

He could see the edge of the palisade outlined faintly against the night. He relaxed as he looked at the one obstacle that barred him from freedom. Four men had circumvented that obstacle successfully; what they had done, he could do also. He rested against the edge of the door and revived his hopes, letting the sight of the palisade drive the phantasms of fear from his mind. He stood a long time before he gained the courage to return to his pile of straw.

*   *   *   *   *

Patrick opened his eyes reluctantly. The morning was wet and gloomy. Victoricus stood over him, shaking him until he muttered, "I'm awake." He stood up and stretched but felt the scars pull across his back and dropped his arms quickly.

The Roman saw the twinge of pain. "Do you want me to bring food?"

Patrick shook his head quickly in refusal. He did not want to become more indebted to the other. He must regain his independence and hold himself apart before gratitude dissuaded him from the escape which would bring ten lashes on the Roman's back.

They walked across the enclosure without talking, hunching their shoulders against the rain. Victoricus guided the way knowingly into a passage between two buildings; before them was a group of perhaps forty men and a very small number of women, crowded together beneath a shelter open on three sides. The fourth side was a huge, open fireplace where two iron cauldrons hung suspended over the flames. "The dining salon," Victoricus muttered bitterly.

Patrick looked curiously at the gathering. He had not had reason to consider the number of slaves in Master Miliucc's establishment; he was surprised at the great number. Only fourteen had been present at the Mass. He saw Father Alexius, but the priest stared warningly that he should not recognize him.

Victoricus muttered indistinctly, as though speaking without moving his lips. "Those two at the right are guards waiting to count us."

They joined the group and stood silently. A few more hurried through the rain. A guard shouted, and the slaves formed into two lines to be counted. Victoricus pointed the place where Patrick was to stand. The guards walked slowly before the two lines, noted the four unoccupied places without apparent interest, then signaled that the group could eat.

Few spoke. All seemed intent on eating as quickly as they could and separating from the others, hurrying away through the rain to whatever task was given them. Some of the men were young, but many others were not; Patrick wondered how long they had endured before they had lost all spirit and all will to escape. Victoricus nudged him as by accident, but Patrick interested himself in the last of his food and let the other walk away alone. Some day

Victoricus might be among these older slaves, living only to regret his lack of courage.

But Victoricus did not lack courage; he had proved that by entering Master Miliucc's house. Patrick watched the Roman disappear around the corner of a building. If not courage, what did the man lack? He put his wooden bowl and spoon where the others had already made a mound in the middle of the shelter and followed after Victoricus.

Victoricus was already working—in his usual inept way, Patrick observed. The Roman youth strained as he dragged a great bundle of straw which he could have rolled across the stable with little effort. Automatically Patrick opened his mouth to suggest the easier method, then changed his purpose; he would let Victoricus be responsible for the stable, as for himself. "What do you want me to do?"

Victoricus finished his task, straightened and looked at Patrick suspiciously. "You know what must be done in a stable. Do whatever you want."

Patrick began to clean a vacant stall, piling the old straw into a corner. His tool struck metal, and he searched about in the straw until he found it—a straight, flat blade, apparently broken from some tool. He tossed it without interest into the open area behind him, but Victoricus approached immediately and recovered it.

"This could be made into a knife," the Roman proposed. Patrick regarded him questioningly. "We need knives, arrowheads, weapons of every kind," Victoricus explained irritably.

"You do intend to escape?" Patrick demanded.

"I've already told you that."

Patrick nodded his head. "When God wills." He had intended to speak mockingly, but the words sounded almost as resigned as when Victoricus spoke them. He scraped straw along the floor toward the pile in the corner. He did not want to return to thoughts of God's will and the torments inseparable from those thoughts.

"We can do what is in our power to prepare," Victoricus insisted.

Patrick stopped the pretense of working and darted a finger toward the piece of metal. "How can you make a knife of that?" he demanded.

"I'll rub it on stone," Victoricus answered.

Patrick looked at him incredulously. The Roman must certainly be the scion of a great and privileged family: only such a one could have the courage of this man, yet be completely ignorant of other matters. "That metal must be heated in a fire and hammered on a forge," he objected.

Victoricus turned the metal about in his hand, examining it uncertainly. "It can't be shaped by rubbing it on stone?"

Patrick heard the Roman's disappointment and sympathized with him. He took the metal and examined it as though to be certain of his pronouncement. "That's tempered, Victoricus," he explained. "It can be worked again only by being heated." He returned the metal to the older youth.

Victoricus studied the metal briefly before dropping it to the ground where Patrick had thrown it. He returned to the front of the stable.

Patrick regulated his efforts, doing as much as his father's workers would do. He must avoid attracting attention by doing too much or too little; he must become a mere appendage so that no one would watch him.

Dann, with another of Master Miliucc's lackeys, entered the stable during the morning to inspect the building and the two at their work; the big overseer stamped about, ranting disagreeably at the disorder of the stable and the worthlessness of the two assigned to care for it. He saw the discarded piece of metal and reached down quickly. "Who had this," he demanded.

Patrick indicated the stable where he had been working. "I found it in the straw," he explained.

"No slave can have metal in his possession," Dann roared threateningly. He enjoyed the opportunity of frightening others if he could. "Take this to the smith," he ordered.

Patrick took the metal. He was glad of an excuse to learn his way about the enclosure and the locations of the buildings. He was most eager to discover where Master Miliucc's ladders were stored.

The rain had stopped but the ground was soft and his feet pressed into the earth. He was careful to walk directly to the smith and follow the same path when he returned. He observed all that he could—the isolation of the smith's building from the others, probably to reduce the danger of conflagration should some mishap occur; he estimated the height of the palisade and knew that, having gained the top by mounting one of Master Miliucc's ladders, he would be able to drop to the ground on the other side without injury; he saw one area where there were no buildings near the palisade and where there would be little danger that any would hear him set a ladder. He could not discover where the ladders were stored; he must find excuses for going to other places within the enclosure until he found it.

He had nearly completed his errand and was about to enter the stable when he saw Master Miliucc with Dann and some others grouped together near the great gates, apparently examining something on the ground. He saw Master

Miliucc step back from the group, survey the whole of his establishment thoughtfully, then speak to Dann. Immediately Dann began to roar a summons to all slaves. Patrick turned but slowed his steps until Victoricus joined him.

Master Miliucc had drawn apart from and somewhat behind his overseer; Dann indicated that the slaves should gather before him. The overseer assumed the posture of a triumphant man, his feet spread far apart and his hands clenched on his hips. On the wet ground in front of him was a small mound covered with a cow hide. He waited with unusual patience until the slaves were assembled.

"Last night," he addressed them sharply, "four men put a ladder against the palisade and escaped—or thought they would escape. Master Miliucc was very angry when he learned of them—he even spoke of putting the lash to all of you to discourage you from following after the four. But the lash prevents men from working—isn't that so, Patrick?— and I asked that he spare all of you." He grinned wickedly at his evil generosity. "I knew those men would return. Now they have returned." He gestured to two men standing directly before him. "Strip off that hide!" he ordered.

The two slaves pulled the hide from the mound; the group pressed forward curiously. Patrick looked down on a tangled mass that was hardly recognizable as the blood-stained clothing and torn flesh of human beings. Someone groaned. Some others retched, nauseated by the sight. Patrick wanted to back away, but he forced himself to stand and look closely. He wanted to remember always what men—barbaric Irishmen—had done to the four; he wanted to hate the barbaric people who would practice such savagery. He felt Victoricus pull at his sleeve and he turned away; most of the others had already fled the scene. He walked with the Roman to the stable, grabbed a forked tool and plunged it angrily into the ground. "People who would do that to other humans are not human themselves. They're savages!" he exclaimed.

"People? The Irish didn't do that, Patrick," Victoricus disagreed. "Wolves attacked those four." Patrick raised his head quickly to dispute the statement, but Victoricus continued immediately. "I've seen the remains of others torn by wolves just as these men were."

"They were stabbed and mutilated by the Irish," Patrick maintained stubbornly.

Victoricus shook his head firmly. "Any Irish who intercepted them would have kept them or would have brought them back here and claimed some reward." Patrick turned away but the older youth followed. "Patrick, can't you see now the need for weapons and waiting for an opportunity to escape? These four fled without weapons or any other preparation. If the wolves had not killed them, they probably would have been retaken by some Irish or would have died of starvation."

Patrick turned about suddenly. "Weapons and other preparations," he repeated angrily. "We can't keep even a broken piece of metal and you talk of weapons."

"When God gives us the opportunity to escape," Victoricus persuaded, "He will give us all else that is necessary."

Patrick wanted to answer jeeringly—wanted to scoff at the other's complaisance; but the seed of doubt, planted during the night, had rooted itself and grown swiftly, even as he had looked down on the remains of the four who had sought their freedom. He began work, striving to dispel the doubt. "God willed all of us to be made captives," Father Alexius' voice echoed again. "He does not shout nor reveal

His anger and thus frighten men to obey Him. Perhaps He should; then men would strive more diligently to know Him and His power, and would obey Him more quickly." The more vigorously he worked, the louder did the words resound in his memory.

He rested little during the nights that followed. He lay awake for long hours, then slept a troubled sleep. In the week, two more slaves, undeterred by the fate of the four, scaled the palisade. Irish captured them and returned them; and Dann summoned all the slaves to watch while he himself administered ten lashes, using all of his brutal strength and skill to tear the flesh from their backs. Patrick's hours of wakefulness lengthened, and his hours of sleep became more troubled.

He knew and admitted the power he confronted. "God willed all of us to be made captives." He could continue stubbornly to resist submission to the fate imposed upon him, but he would not stupidly deny that it had been imposed on him. "God willed . . ." Slowly and grudgingly he retreated. He could not doubt nor even dismiss the thought that God had indeed willed him to be made a captive; how else could it have happened? He confronted the choice of submitting to the divine decree, as Victoricus did, or continuing to struggle—probably in vain—to escape.

He surprised Father Alexius by appearing at the next Mass celebrated by the priest, and he confirmed the surprise by attending another Mass celebrated two weeks later. He acknowledged the hopelessness of pitting his strength against the will of the all-powerful God and, for the first time, experienced fear of the Supreme Being who could subject him to punishment through all future ages of time and eternity as readily as He had thrust him into this pit of deprivation. In the third month of his life as a slave at Slemish, Patrick knelt before Father Alexius in a dark storage shed, heard the words of absolution that freed him from the past and strengthened him for the future, attended the Mass, and received Holy Communion.

"And there in Ireland," Patrick wrote in his *Confession,* "the Lord opened the sense of my unbelief so that at last I remembered my sins and, remembering them, turned to Him with all my heart. God pitied my abjection, had mercy on my youth and ignorance, then comforted me as a father would his son."

4

FROM his sixteenth to his nineteenth year, 401 to 404, Patrick became in stature the man his youth had promised. He grew taller than Victoricus and broad-shouldered. His muscles developed as long cords along his flat, heavy bones so that, despite his tremendous strength, he retained a deceptive appearance of slenderness together with a quickness of movement unusual in a powerful man.

Interiorly, he changed even more remarkably. Self-centeredness, with its concomitant selfishness, disappeared; contempt for the weakness of others became a willingness to assist so that he took upon himself the more arduous tasks in the stable and left the lighter work to Victoricus. His intense aloofness gave way to friendliness.

Temperament alone remained what it had always been. He was hard and inflexible. Having committed himself to a course of action, he pursued it unwaveringly and unremittingly. He established within himself a concept of God and God's rights and God's powers as the one, absolute certainty, then exerted himself to establish the same concept in the other enslaved Britons until nearly all attended Father Alexius' Masses regularly. He admitted no exceptions nor opposed concepts and, consequently, suffered none of the periods of depression, despair or doubt which periodically assailed Victoricus.

"You have no imagination," Victoricus discovered. "You never worry about tomorrow or the next day or the day after."

Patrick shrugged aside the comment unconcernedly. He cared not at all whether he had or had not imagination. He had surrendered freely and willingly to God, so he had surrendered completely. Tomorrow and the next day and the day after were within God's realm, not his. "If I concern myself about the future," he analyzed, "then I am no longer submitting to God's will but following my own."

Victoricus looked at him strangely, obviously impressed. "You are learning the Irish tongue," he reminded him.

"Because you and Father Alexius said that learning Irish is a necessary part of preparing," Patrick answered. He smiled grimly. "I would never learn it for any reason of my own."

On the night when he had knelt beside Father Alexius and confessed his sins, he had put completely from him all intent to escape until God Himself afforded the opportunity. He had seen where Master Miliucc's ladders were stored, but he felt no temptation to make use of them. From time to time, others escaped; but only two disappeared permanently. The rest returned—the living to be scourged, the dead to be displayed as a deterrent to others. Neither the presumed success of the two nor the failure of the others affected Patrick. He had asserted his submission to the Divine will; he awaited expression of it.

A new companion joined them in the beginning of the fourth year at Slemish. On a day in the fall of 404, a man's angry cursing and a dog's anguished howl sounded simultaneously in the enclosure. Patrick glanced out of the stable; he saw Master Miliucc, then Dann, then others kick brutally at a young dog that dodged away from each one only to encounter a blow from another. At last the dog escaped the group and ran fearfully across the open enclosure.

Impulsively, Patrick crouched down within the doorway and snapped his fingers at the frightened animal. Trustingly, despite the treatment received from the others, the dog swerved from its path and ran into Patrick's welcoming arms.

The feel of the coarse hair in his hands or the trustfulness of the animal or both threatened momentarily to overwhelm Patrick. A hard lump choked him; if he closed his eyes, the years would disappear and he would be again at Bannaventa with Coco.

Victoricus stopped his work and joined them. He stooped down to rub his hand over the head of the dog, adding his assurance that the new arrival was welcome. He laughed. "You've found one Irishman you can like, Patrick. You've acquired an Irish wolfhound."

"An entertainer," Patrick corrected quickly. "All dogs are entertainers—isn't that so, Irish?"

The dog drew his head back and studied Patrick comically, his head tilted sharply.

"But you understand only Irish," Patrick sympathized. He spoke haltingly in the strange tongue he was learning laboriously, and the dog responded immediately by leaping at him playfully.

Victoricus laughed at the dog's eager friendliness. "He can teach you the language while you teach him Latin."

Patrick returned to his work, pleasantly aware of the dog's presence. He watched it briefly as it investigated curiously the horses in their stalls, but both horses and dog seemed to accept each other without difficulty.

Another visitor arrived soon after the dog, a boy who stopped just inside the door. He entered so quietly that neither Patrick nor Victoricus, concentrating on their tasks, were aware of his presence until the dog leaped joyfully toward him. The boy dropped to his knees, hugged the squirming animal, and murmured softly in a needless effort to comfort it for the kicks it had already forgotten.

Patrick watched the scene uneasily. He knew the boy as Dichu, a ward of Master Miliucc under that peculiar custom these Irish practiced of placing their twelve-year-old boys in the home of an important man. The boy had arrived a week earlier at the home of the lord of Slemish; slaves employed in the household reported that he was the son of a man who was honored that the great lord had accepted his son.

Dichu looked gravely at Patrick. "I am grateful to you," he said in Irish; but the harsh language seemed to soften as he uttered it. "I was on the other side of the enclosure when I saw you call my dog."

Patrick did not answer. He resented the boy both because he was Irish and because he would take the dog away from the stable.

The dog squirmed free of the crouching boy, then leaped on him and knocked him backwards. Patrick walked forward and was rewarded by a charging leap of welcome from the dog. "You should train your dog not to leap, Master Dichu. That is why the men kicked at him."

The boy sat up eagerly. "I do train him," he asserted, "but he learns only what he wants to learn."

"He will learn if you teach him firmly," Patrick admonished.

Dichu studied Patrick doubtfully. "I can't hurt him." His tone warned that he would not permit others to hurt his pet. He was satisfied with Patrick's brusque nod of agreement. "Master Miliucc doesn't like him," he confided. "He will not allow me to keep him in the house any longer."

Victoricus joined them, looking down on the crouching man and boy, each of whom fondled the well-pleased dog that stood contentedly between them. "You could leave your dog here, Master Dichu, with Patrick. He could teach you how to train him."

The boy's doleful expression disappeared immediately and completely. He looked hopefully at Patrick. "Will you?" he asked.

Patrick looked up at Victoricus. "This boy is Irish," he said harshly, in Latin.

"So is the dog," the Roman countered. "You like the dog. If you want to keep him here, you must pay some price for the privilege. If you teach Dichu how to train his dog, Miliucc will put the boy to breeding and training other dogs for sale while this one stays with you."

"What are you saying? What is that language?" Dichu interrupted.

Victoricus avoided the first question by answering the second. "You should learn Latin, Master Dichu," he continued. "Those who breed these dogs train them to obey Latin commands so that they can sell them in Rome."

The name puzzled Dichu. "Is that in Ireland?"

"Far away, Master Dichu," Victoricus answered. His expression changed rapidly as he realized the significance of his own words. He looked down at the dog then at Patrick. "Sometimes it seems very far away." He turned suddenly and walked into the depths of the stable.

Dichu noted nothing unusual in the manner of Victoricus. He looked at Patrick. "I won't sell Tulchann," he declared. The dog turned his head alertly at the sound of his name.

Despite his aversion, Patrick nodded approvingly. "He likes that name, Master Dichu."

"I won't sell him," the boy repeated belligerently.

Patrick stood up. The dog leaped against him, then against Dichu. Patrick moved his head slowly. "He wouldn't let you sell him, Master Dichu. He wouldn't stay with anyone but you."

Dichu smiled. "He stayed with you," he observed generously. "Will you keep him and teach me to train him?"

Patrick looked at the dog and felt himself weakening. Deliberately he turned his attention from the dog to the Irish boy. He could not dislike the dog; he could dislike the boy who was Irish.

Dichu leaped up without waiting for an answer. "I will ask Master Miliucc," he said eagerly. He hauled the dog to Patrick. "Hold him so that he can't follow me. I will ask Master Miliucc now." He hurried out of the stable, closing the door carefully behind him.

The lord of Slemish came to the stable that same afternoon, preceded by Dann who called Patrick and Victoricus to stand respectfully by the door while their master was present. The big overseer glowered menacingly, ignorant of the matter that had prompted Miliucc to this unprecedented visit to the stable but ready to inflict any punishment imposed on the two. Tulchann cowered into the darkness at the far end of the stable.

Patrick stood where he had been directed, his hands behind him, clenching, unclenching, engaging and separating, in an attempt to dissipate his hatred. It was the one weakness he had to review repeatedly with Father Alexius, one he could not conquer. "They are like beasts," he excused himself to the priest. "They are all barbarians." Now he watched covertly as the two walked half the length of the stable; he averted his eyes as they returned.

"You have learned our Irish language?" Master Miliucc demanded of Patrick.

Patrick forced his voice to be respectful. "Somewhat, Master." He could not look at the man.

"You will keep that dog," the lord of Slemish ordered, "and teach Master Dichu to train him. If the boy learns well, he will breed dogs for sale at Rome." He turned and left the stable abruptly; Dann hurried after him.

Victoricus breathed a deep sigh of relief. He stepped to the doorway to be certain that the two had departed, then shook his head wonderingly. "I can never forget how his two little girls welcomed him the day he brought us here—and never understand how they can love such a monster."

Tulchann emerged from his refuge, leaped against Patrick, then stood and pawed at him for attention. Patrick rubbed the dog's ears absently. He was tensely angry. "They can never let us forget what we are. 'Keep that dog! Teach Master Dichu to train him!'" he repeated Miliucc's words. "They make what could be a pleasure into another task for the slave."

Young Dichu returned in the late hours of the afternoon, eager to begin immediately, but Patrick refused. "I have other work," he said curtly. The anger incited by Miliucc and Dann tended to include the boy also, as though Dichu's status of ward made him one with the older pair.

The boy did not insist. He stooped down and occupied

himself with the playful Tulchann as though inured to rejection by many previous experiences. "You will be good to Tulchann?" he asked after a time.

Patrick heard a note in the boy's voice which should never be present in the voice of a twelve-year-old. Was it resignation or hopelessness or defeat? It seemed almost to announce that the one certainty in this boy's life was the mutual affection between himself and his dog.

Patrick fought down the surge of sympathy. The boy was merely another of these barbarous Irish. In time he would become callous and hardened, would become a barbarian who shouted taunts at captives as the people of the villages did; he might even become as cruel and brutal as Miliucc and Dann.

"I'll care for Tulchann," he answered roughly without looking at the boy. He heard Dichu and Tulchann at the stable door, heard the door close, then felt the dog again beside him. He leaned down, petted the dog, then straightened to continue his work but saw Victoricus looking at him.

"That boy carries a heavy heart, Patrick."

Patrick shrugged his shoulders.

*   *   *   *   *

Dichu came again very early in the morning. He did not interrupt Patrick and Victoricus at their work but sat down near the door and waited patiently, wrestling with Tulchann and talking to him.

For a time Patrick watched the two while he continued his own work. The night had not lessened his resentment against Master Miliucc's order, but it had diminished his antipathy to the boy; he felt it vanishing completely as he watched Dichu and his dog. He did not want to lose his aversion, he knew; yet he did want the companionship of the dog and must pay the price required to gain it. He walked to the front of the stable, and Tulchann welcomed him by leaping against him.

Patrick grasped the dog's paws and held him upright. "First, you will teach Tulchann not to leap against you," he instructed impersonally. He stepped on the dog's back paw and Tulchann dropped immediately to the ground.

"That hurts him," Dichu protested.

Tulchann leaped again at Patrick and Patrick repeated the action. "You would rather that Master Miliucc and the others kick him?" he asked irritably. "You needn't press on his paw," he explained. "Touch his foot with yours."

Dichu moved and the dog leaped against him. Gently the boy put his foot on Tulchann's back paw, and Tulchann dropped down immediately. "That doesn't hurt him, does it?" The boy smiled slightly.

From that first day, Patrick felt his reserve crumbling before Dichu's trustful confidence. It was, he thought, the same quality utilized by dogs to win the affection of men. Only a man confirmed in brutality—a man such as Master Miliucc or Dann—could withhold affection when pressed by a child or animal.

Boy and dog progressed together. Early in November they delighted each other when Tulchann learned to sit up straight at Dichu's command with his forepaws close to his chest. On that day, Patrick joined in Dichu's delighted laughter for the first time; on that day he abandoned the last remnants of his antipathy to the boy.

Soon after that achievement, Dichu brought as specta-tors the two small daughters of Master Miliucc to watch the slave who could teach dogs to do many incredible things. The two watched very briefly before their attention was diverted by the efforts of Victoricus to put a bridle over the head of a colt. They wandered farther into the interior of the stable for a better view.

Victoricus rested a short time between each attempt to bridle the colt but continued to talk soothingly to the nervous animal.

"Can you talk to horses?"

Victoricus looked down at the serious-faced questioner and nodded soberly. "I tell him to keep his head still while I put his hat on him."

The older, Eilethe, studied Victoricus doubtfully until she discovered his humor. She laughed; then, without more cause, both children began to shriek delightedly. After that day, Dichu never appeared without the two smaller children, who went immediately to Victoricus while he and Patrick drilled Tulchann.

Occasionally Patrick heard Victoricus entertaining the younger children with tales of other children in "lands far away—over the sea." At times, under pretense of resting Tulchann, both he and Dichu listened to the older youth. On a day late in December, he heard Victoricus tell the story of the little boy who was born in a stable "just like this" and listened raptly but fearfully as the other related the story of the Nativity. He glanced at Dichu: The boy was transported, oblivious to all else but the voice of Victoricus. As soon as the recital ended, Patrick announced noisily that he and Victoricus had work to do and the children must find other amusements.

"If the children repeat that story," he observed when the three had gone, "someone may recognize it."

Victorian nodded indifferently. "I didn't intend to tell that story to them, but I couldn't help myself. It almost seemed as though God wanted them to know the story of the Nativity."

When the three came again on the following day, Eilethe demanded immediately "another story about Jesus."

Patrick saw Victoricus' discomfiture. "Tell them of Herod and the Innocents," he suggested impulsively. He was startled by his own boldness, then strangely pleased with himself.

Inevitably, Victoricus' recital touched on angels, and he was required to explain the invisible beings who served God as messengers or served men as guardians.

"We have angels," Eilethe volunteered, "but they are not messengers or guardians. They live together in great palaces under hills . . ."

"They are fairies," Dichu called out scornfully. His interest in the training of Tulchann languished. "But we have a god, Victoricus. He is Cenn Cruaich at Mag Slecht." He stood erect, swelled his chest, and flexed his arms demonstratively. "He is a great bronze god surrounded by smaller gods of stone."

The stable was very quiet for a moment, then Victoricus began a story devoid of angels and God. Dichu left Patrick and joined the other group. "Is your God like Cenn Cruaich?" he asked.

Patrick watched Victoricus. The Roman hesitated, as though deciding whether to answer the question or launch some distraction. "Can you love Cenn Cruaich, Dichu?" Patrick called.

Dichu turned and shook his head quickly in denial. He assumed an expression of awe. "I'm afraid of him," he admitted.

Patrick smiled confidently. "Then Cenn Cruaich is not like our God. We love our God and our God loves us."

Victoricus terminated the session before Dichu could continue the conversation. "We have work to do now." He shepherded the children to the door, despite Eilethe's protests, and urged them gently from the stable. "We may be advancing them too rapidly, Patrick."

"Not Dichu."

"Not Dichu," Victoricus agreed. "Dichu has so much confidence in you that he is eager to believe whatever you tell him. But Eilethe was baffled by the thought that there was some God other than Cenn Cruaich. In the future, I think I had better take Eilethe and her sister farther away from you and Dichu. You can talk to Dichu while I talk to the little ones."

Patrick laughed suddenly. "Father Alexius may have a few baptisms that he never expected."

Their plans and expectations were vain. They were awakened during the night by Tulchann's growling, then heard Dichu quieting the dog. The boy had come with the news that they were discovered. In quick, nervous words, he reported that Eilethe had innocently repeated Patrick's statements about God. "Then Master Miliucc questioned her, and she told him what you told us about Jesus."

"He didn't punish her?" Victoricus inquired.

"He wouldn't punish Eilethe, Victoricus," Dichu answered. "But he was very frightened—either of Cenn Cruaich or of your God—I don't know which. He started to rage and told Dann to scourge both of you. That made Eilethe and her sister cry, and they begged him not to hurt either of you. Then he told Dann to separate you. Patrick, you are to be a shepherd, and Victoricus, you are to work for the smith."

Patrick grappled with an undefined premonition, as though the boy had conveyed some message not contained in his words. He arose completely from the straw, trying to grasp and understand the hidden meaning.

Victoricus laughed softly in the darkness. "I never thought of myself as a smith. What makes Master Miliucc think me capable of forging, Dichu?"

Dichu hesitated and his voice was uncertain when he answered. "I think he wants to put you and your God under the smith's spell; all smiths can cast spells," he added.

"You don't really believe that, do you, Dichu," Victoricus chided lightly. "I promise that the smith won't be able to cast a spell on me—you will see, Dichu, how strong my God is."

"I won't be here, Victoricus," the boy answered. "Master Miliucc is sending me back to my father." His voice wavered between dejection and gladness; he regretted departure from his friends while welcoming return to his father.

The boy's statement recalled Patrick's attention from the thought that had claimed it. He had not realized the extent of his affection for this Irish boy—an affection he thought impossible. He had not realized the extent of his hope that this boy would be baptized. Now he realized both in the sadness that pressed against him.

"Dichu," Patrick called, "we told you very little about God; but God will teach you about Himself if you will think of Him as your Creator. He made you—He made each of us so we should always be grateful to Him for giving us life. Think of Him as our Creator and the Creator of everything in the world. If you will do that, He will tell you more about Himself."

"How?" the boy demanded.

"I don't know, Dichu. I do know that He will teach you if you tell Him you want to know Him."

"I will," the boy promised hurriedly. "Will you be able to keep Tulchann while you are a shepherd?" he asked anxiously.

Patrick reached out into the darkness until his hand found Dichu's shoulder and grasped it firmly. "You will take Tulchann, Dichu." He forced himself to laugh lightly. "Four or five other dogs will be with me to care for the sheep. But don't change him again into an Irish-speaking dog."

"I'll train all my dogs with Latin words," said Dichu. His hand grasped Patrick's. "I must go back to the house. Goodbye, Patrick. Goodbye, Victoricus. They won't let me see you tomorrow."

Despite the impenetrable darkness, he seemed almost to run from the stable, stopping only to caution Tulchann not to follow him.

"I suppose I should have been more prudent," Victoricus said regretfully.

"I wonder," Patrick countered.

"About prudence?"

"I wonder if God isn't using our lack of prudence as a means for moving us nearer to escape?"

"What are you thinking?" Victoricus demanded.

"I am remembering," Patrick explained. "I remember that we have been praying for the opportunity to escape. I remember that we have tried to prepare ourselves for that opportunity by learning the Irish language. I realize now that we have learned that language very well from talking to these children during the last few months." The thought that had started as a premonition grew clearer in his mind.

"I remember, too, that we agreed we should need weapons both to protect ourselves and to obtain food after we escaped from Slemish; and now God is putting you into the very place—the one place where those weapons can be made."

"Patrick," Victoricus said slowly and emphatically, "you will be given some weapon—at least a heavy knife and a shepherd's crook. You are not to wait until I have an opportunity to join you. When you know that you have the opportunity to escape, then go!"

Patrick made his voice equally firm and emphatic. "While you make weapons, Victoricus, I'll pray. I don't believe that the God we love and Who loves us would give me an opportunity to escape without giving it to you also. I will not leave Slemish without you."

5

THE nineteen-year-old Patrick who emerged from Master Miliucc's establishment carried within himself secrets he had not suspected when he entered it as a sixteen-year-old. He had learned to know God, he knew the inner invisible change wrought within himself by God, he could distinguish the precise steps by which God had accomplished the change and taught him of Himself. It was the knowledge of those secrets that had prompted him to tell Victoricus, "While you make weapons, I'll pray."

He fulfilled his promise to the Roman in the same tenacious manner he did everything. "I prayed as I tended sheep," he wrote in his *Confession,* "whether I was in the valleys or on the mountains. I would rise to pray before daylight, even though snow or frost or rain fell upon the earth, because there was no sloth in me. The love of God and His fear came more and more upon me to strengthen my faith."

He saw the physical resemblance of his work as shepherd to the spiritual work of the Divine Master, the Good Shepherd; he did not presume to see any greater resemblance. He was consoled, he was comforted, he was strengthened. "My spirit was moved so that I would say a hundred prayers or more each day and as many at night."

His cross during the three years from 404 to 407 was a complex of uncertainty and loneliness. He was confident of ultimate deliverance from the Irish, but he was tormented by the uncertain length of time he must endure; he lived through long periods when he did not see another human. When he did encounter other shepherds—all Irish—he welcomed them for the relief from loneliness and remained several days with them.

For a time, separation from Victoricus was his heaviest burden. At the lambing season and, again, at the shearing season, when he drove the sheep into the village below Master Miliucc's establishment, he sought an excuse for reentering the hated enclosure on the hilltop but failed. On the lonely hillsides, he wondered whether he was anxious for the welfare of Victoricus or merely desirous of learning of the Roman's handiwork.

Four dogs were his companions. They were surly and dispirited and poorly trained in the beginning, and he amused himself—and the dogs—by training them in their work, then training them to perform artfully. He trained them also to work in unison so that when one sounded an alarm, the others raced to assist against wolves attempting to raid the flock.

On a night in January of 407, when he had guided the flock within sight of the village, he was awakened by the barking of one dog, followed immediately by the barking of the others as they hurried against an enemy. The night was cold and Patrick looked out reluctantly from his small shelter on the snow-covered earth that lay bright beneath a great moon.

He heard a new sound mingling with the snarling and barking of the dogs—a low, rumbling growl. The enemy was not the usual pack of wolves! Patrick snatched up his crook and ran across the level area where the sheep huddled.

In the moonlight, he could see the dogs leaping forward and back, growling and snarling fiercely as they fought. As he neared the site, he saw a great, shaggy beast sitting back on its haunches, striking with its upraised forepaws as the dogs feinted or attacked. One of the dogs was already sprawled dead on the ground, but the other three held faithfully to their task. Patrick had never seen a bear, but he recognized the animal from the descriptions men had given—men who had not minimized their fear of the animal.

His approach seemed to incite the dogs to new efforts. One maneuvered behind the bear, then leaped against the unprotected back, clamping his teeth tightly on the scruff of the neck. The bear pawed ineffectually at his tormentor and screamed fearsomely. The other dogs leaped upward, raking their teeth deeply into the bear. Patrick charged forward recklessly, leveling the sharp point of the crook at the beast's throat, throwing the weight of his body into the thrust that pierced hide and flesh and made the animal leap upward into the air.

Patrick felt a stunning pain across his chest, a searing burn where the bear's paws tore cloth and flesh together. He fell and rolled clear of the animal threshing about in the snow. He struggled to his feet, clutching his knife; he wondered at the weakness that assailed him and prevented him from moving quickly when opportunity offered. He could only watch the dogs leap and tear at their fallen foe while its lifeblood flowed from the gaping wound in its throat and blotched the clean snow. The bear lay still at last, and the dogs sank down, worn and tired.

Patrick called them. He would also have liked to lie down and rest in the cold snow but knew that he dare not;

someone must attend his wounded chest, and someone must care for the sheep in his stead. He sent the dogs circling to bring the flock together and drive it toward the village.

He had proceeded a very little distance when a man of the village approached, apparently attracted by the sounds of the conflict. The man did not require an explanation—Patrick's bloodstained and torn clothing were sufficient. He, a much smaller man, drew Patrick's arm over his shoulder and aided him the remaining distance to the nearest house.

The house was small and warm; a fire burned in the fireplace. Patrick felt the muscles of his body relax as he lay on the couch where the man placed him. It had been long since he had felt such warmth. "The sheep," he muttered guiltily.

The man—Patrick saw that he was young as himself—brought a thick candle he had lighted at the fire. "The sheep are outside," he assured. "The dogs will care for them until I can."

Patrick closed his eyes contentedly. He heard the other adding wood to the fire and pouring water into the pot over the flames.

He opened his eyes again when the villager started to draw the torn clothing gently from the wound.

"I am Patrick," he offered. "I am one of Master Miliucc's slaves."

The villager nodded. "I am Erc." He displayed no interest in Patrick's status. He was absorbed in the task of washing the wound, then of applying an ointment from an earthen vessel.

The ointment stung the raw flesh and Patrick flinched. "Your ointment is good," he gritted.

Erc's blue eyes glinted admiringly at his humor. "It stings," he admitted. He wound a long length of cloth about Patrick's chest. "Some of your ribs are broken," he announced authoritatively.

"A bear," Patrick explained. He saw immediately that the single word alarmed Erc. "He's dead," he added quickly. The young man probably had his own sheep exposed in the fields.

Erc's smile returned quickly. "Bear meat is good; I'll go out and bring him back before Master Miliucc sends some of his men." He worked steadily at the task of winding the cloth about Patrick's chest until he was satisfied. "Sleep," he told Patrick. "I will get the bear."

Daylight was filtering through the small window openings high in the wall of Erc's house when Patrick awakened. He heard voices outside the door and recognized Erc's.

"I went out myself," Erc was saying argumentatively. "The bear was dead. This man's crook was driven through its neck. See for yourself. No!" he raised his voice quickly, "he could not have thrown it. I tell you he had to hold the crook and drive it against the bear's throat to do it."

"He's a slave," another voice disparaged. "No slave would do that for sheep."

"This slave, Patrick, did," Erc retorted heatedly. "He saved Master Miliucc's sheep and ours also." He came into the house, closing the door quickly but softly behind him, too annoyed to continue the conversation. He glanced toward Patrick, evidently expecting that he would be sleeping; he was surprised that he was awake. "You heard?" he asked uncomfortably, walking to the couch.

Patrick moved his head slightly. "I heard," he answered coldly. Once, when he had first seen this village, he had realized that the people were not friends of Master Miliucc, and he had hoped their attitude might be different from that of the other villages.

"My father and mother were slaves," Erc volunteered defensively. "These villagers think that is a reproach."

Patrick looked at him with new interest. "You are not Irish?" he asked hopefully.

The question surprised Erc. "I am Irish. My parents were from the west country—from Connaught. They were captured and brought here during one of the wars between the Connaughtmen and these Ulstermen."

"Why didn't they escape?"

"My father could have, but he wouldn't leave without my mother." He jerked his head to indicate Master Miliucc's establishment. "They were held in the enclosure, but Master Miliucc's father freed them before he died and gave them this house."

"He was more generous than his son will ever be," Patrick said bitterly.

Erc sat down on the side of the couch. "Master Miliucc was not always as he is now," he said slowly. "One of the women slaves killed his wife—stabbed her not long after their second little girl was born. He changed after that— began to treat all slaves as animals."

A noise outside the house interrupted them. Voices increased rapidly; the entire village seemed aroused. The door burst open and Dann entered, slamming the door behind him to shut out any who thought to follow. "Get up!" he ordered sharply from the doorway.

Erc had moved toward the door. His slight form seemed to stiffen as he confronted the big overseer. "He can't get up," he answered immediately, "and our law protects a slave who has been injured."

Dann strode toward the couch, pretending to ignore the small man, but Erc moved quickly in front of him.

"The law requires that a wounded slave be treated and healed."

Dann scowled. "Master Miliucc will treat and heal him."

Erc grinned impudently. "He will be moved to the enclosure when I say he can be moved. The law so provides."

Patrick recognized the opportunity for which he had waited. He struggled to rise from the couch but Erc moved to him quickly and restrained him. "I will not burden you," Patrick complained. He must seize this opportunity of reentering the enclosure.

Erc pressed against his shoulders until Patrick relaxed. "You are not a burden. Master Miliucc must pay for your care."

"Master Miliucc will pay you for no more than one day," Dann decreed. He turned about and hurried through the door before Erc could reply.

"He will pay for as many days as necessary," Erc muttered.

Patrick closed his eyes and lay quietly, exhausted by the effort to rise and the pain that had accompanied it. After a time he heard the door close softly and knew that Erc had gone out. He must persuade Erc to take him to the enclosure long before he was healed—he had waited three years for this opportunity of seeing Victoricus again and must not lose it. He thought of excuses he might use but saw immediately the transparency of each. He realized that he must tell Erc truthfully his desire of reentering the enclosure on the hilltop. The resolution quieted him and he slept until the other returned.

Erc listened patiently as Patrick told of his friend and his desire to see him again; but he studied Patrick more intently as he understood. "You have made some plans to escape—planned together," he said knowingly. "Is that it, Patrick?" He didn't wait for an answer. "Don't attempt it," he cautioned soberly, "and tell your friend not to attempt it. No one ever escapes. Some are caught and returned for the reward; most are caught by wolves."

"We are not planning to escape now," Patrick said carefully.

"Now or at any time, Patrick—people and wolves do not change because of time."

Patrick knew the danger of confiding in the Irishman; he weighed the danger against the desire of seeing Victoricus again. He must accept some risk, he decided, and this man was more friendly than any other might be. "You said your father remained in slavery only because of your mother, Erc. He didn't want to be a slave. He might have preferred death rather than to continue as a slave had it not been for your mother." He saw Erc's interest and sympathy appear in his expression. He told then of his father and his desire to return to him.

When Patrick finished, Erc looked at him a moment, then drew away from him and turned his back. "You deserve your freedom," he admitted. "You should be given it in return for saving Master Miliucc's sheep. But we know he will never grant that and, if ever . . . A man of your courage might succeed in escaping," he concluded suddenly.

"I do not ask your help," Patrick said quickly. "I only want you to take me to the enclosure before I recover completely so that they must let me remain there a few days."

Erc turned about. The impudent smile had returned. "You deserve something of me, also, Patrick; that bear could have killed many of my sheep. I will take you to Master Miliucc's as soon as you can walk up the hill."

*   *   *   *   *

On the third day and again on the fourth, Patrick succeeded in sitting up on the side of the sleeping couch but, on each occasion, had to lie down again immediately. On the fifth day he was encouraged by a sudden increase of strength that enabled him to remain upright a much longer time. On the seventh day Erc agreed that he might attempt the ascent to the enclosure on the top of the hill, and he produced a crude woolen garment to replace the clothing torn during the encounter with the bear. "Master Miliucc must pay for that also," he assured.

The day was cold and damp; Patrick shivered and drew the woolen cloak closer about him. For a moment he regretted departure from the dry warmth of Erc's house; but he turned his attention quickly to the hope of seeing Victoricus.

They encountered only three men of the village, and those three spoke gruffly to Erc while avoiding Patrick. Their attitude proved sufficiently that they would be glad to intercept and return a slave who escaped, both for the reward and the pleasure they would derive.

The gatemen admitted them to the enclosure but made them wait until one went to Dann for instructions. He returned soon and pointed to a small storage shed which Patrick should use for his quarters. "There is some straw in there," he added, apparently aware of Patrick's injuries. He directed Erc to Master Miliucc's house. "Dann will pay you," he said.

Patrick alternated during that day between the heap of straw where he could rest and the door from which he could observe the enclosure. He could see the entrance to the smith; he tried to see the flour mill, but that building was obscured by others. He examined every figure he saw but found none that resembled either Victoricus or Father Alexius. He was dismayed by the thought that the two might no longer be present, and his anxiety prompted him to go early to the shelter where the slaves received their food.

Victoricus was there! But it was a Victoricus no longer slender and erect. The Roman had become thin and stooped during the three years of their separation, and he coughed frequently. His eyes glittered feverishly, yet beneath the surface glitter Patrick saw the brightness of a deep inner joy.

"You're sick," Patrick said anxiously.

Victoricus nodded almost imperceptibly and without interest. "Do not talk," he cautioned. "I will visit you tonight."

Patrick stifled the questions he wanted to ask. He ate slowly, little interested in the food, watching for Father Alexius. The priest did not appear. "Father Alexius?" he asked softly.

Victoricus did not raise his head. "Killed," he whispered. "A millstone fell on him the day after you left the enclosure." He finished the last of his food, stood up immediately, and walked away.

Patrick forced himself to eat the remainder of his food. During the days and nights on the hills, while he watched the sheep, he had related Victoricus to the idea of eventual escape; but he realized he had hoped that they might persuade Father Alexius to join them—he had even dreamed that he and Victoricus might organize a band to return and rescue the priest. Now the priest was dead—had been dead since he had left the enclosure three years ago. It almost seemed that the two events were related—as though Father Alexius had completed the task God had given him on earth and had left this life as soon as Patrick was removed from his influence.

He thought of the enormity of adversity that had descended upon Victoricus—the sudden change from his status as a privileged young Roman noble to stable slave, then his assignment to the heavy work of the smith, the death of the priest and consequent deprivation of the sacraments. He remembered the uncertainty that had afflicted him and knew it must have been an even greater cross to Victoricus imprisoned in the enclosure. To all this was added illness. By comparison, his own cross had been very light; even the wounds inflicted by the bear became negligible. How could the spirit of joy remain so vibrant in a man so burdened?

The joyfulness was even more evident in Victoricus when he came to the shed, long after darkness and quiet settled over the enclosure, and embraced Patrick. His voice was light and quick, despite the coughing that interrupted him; he was elated that they were reunited once more. "I thought certainly that you had escaped, Patrick," he admitted. "Then I heard the story of your fight with the bear. You should have escaped long ago if you had the opportunity," he scolded.

"I said I would not go without you," Patrick reminded him.

"I'm sick, Patrick," the Roman objected. "This cough," he explained, "and I spit blood. I'm too sick to think any longer of escaping physically. I think God is giving me a better means of escape."

"You're letting your faith weaken," Patrick charged. "God will release us together," he added firmly.

"He may," Victoricus answered without enthusiasm. "But whether we go together or you go alone, these will be necessary." Patrick felt a leather bundle. "What is it?"

"You said I should make weapons while you prayed," Victoricus reminded him. "These are the weapons," he related. "Knives, spearheads, arrowheads—and all of the finest workmanship." He laughed, but the laugh changed again to the racking cough. "Take them with you," he ordered when the spasm ceased. "You can make shafts for spears and arrows."

"Victoricus! I can do that in a few weeks. That will complete our preparations! God must intend to deliver us very soon."

"The language," Victoricus muttered. "I've probably forgotten what I learned from Dichu."

Patrick laughed softly. "I speak it fluently; I've almost forgotten Latin. Victoricus, the only persons to whom I've spoken since I became a shepherd were Irish." His voice trailed away wonderingly. He understood God's design. "I promised to pray, Victoricus, and I did. But God made me lonely so that I would talk to those I met—even to the Irish. So I learned the language very well."

"I hope He doesn't wait . . ." Victoricus began, but a new spasm of coughing interrupted him.

"Just a little longer, Victoricus," Patrick encouraged. "Whether a little or a long time is not important," the Roman answered resignedly.

Patrick's confidence increased steadily. "We need a few more weeks while I make shafts for arrows and spears, Victoricus—and some bows. When I've done that, we will be ready. Then God will give us the opportunity."

They talked some time longer until Patrick decided they must stop. "You must sleep," he urged. "Victoricus, you must rest as much as you can and recover your strength."

"We can talk again tomorrow night," Victoricus proposed.

"We will meet only when we go for food," Patrick decided. He laughed softly at the manner of domination he assumed. "We will have abundant time to talk when we leave Master Miliucc's. You must use your time for rest."

The days passed slowly. Awareness of God's design and of Victoricus' illness made Patrick as impatient to leave the enclosure again as he had been to enter it. Each day, when one of Dann's messengers came to look at his wounds and estimate his recovery, Patrick hoped to be dismissed. When the messenger returned on the eighth day with a brusque order that he return to the sheep, Patrick arose readily. He delayed only long enough to conceal the leather bag under his woolen cloak and flatten it against his body.

The way to the gate led him close to Master Miliucc's house. He was surprised to see Erc, sitting on the ground, but leaning backward against the doorway, his eyes closed as though sleeping. Patrick veered sharply from his path to lead Erc away from the certain anger of Master Miliucc or Dann. "Erc!"

Erc opened his eyes and smiled. "You look completely well again, Patrick."

Patrick nodded then leaned down to grasp the other's arm. "You should not sit here," he cautioned.

Erc was surprised, then grinned confidently. "I'm fasting against Master Miliucc," he explained.

Patrick looked down at him questioningly. He could not understand the strange explanation.

"Master Miliucc has not paid me all he must for caring for you, Patrick—nor for that cloak—as he is required to do by our law. So I am fasting against him," Erc explained. "As long as any freeman fasts against his lord, with a just cause, he disgraces his lord. No other freeman will perform any work for the lord—and I and all the freemen are protected from harm by other laws."

Dann came around the corner of the house and approached belligerently. He ignored Erc but glared at Patrick. "Get out of here!" he roared.

Patrick hurried toward the gate, anxious to be gone from the enclosure with his precious burden before Dann might decide to assign him to work inside. He started down the path to the village, speeding his pace as a new and urgent goal formed in his mind. He would "fast against" God, as Erc fasted against his lord, with just cause; he would fast until God granted the opportunity for which he and Victoricus had prayed so long.

Fast? From what would he fast? Certainly not the poor and insufficient food allotted to a shepherd. He turned the question about in his mind as he hurried through the village to the place where the flock of sheep would be waiting under the care of some villager. From what would he fast? He was within sight of the sheep when he decided that God must decide even that for him and give him even that opportunity.

*   *   *   *   *

Patrick knew the justice of his claim against God, for God Himself had taught men to demand of Him, "Give us this day our daily bread;" not, indeed, as though any man could issue demands against God, but that no man could live without the necessities of life which God alone can give or limit or withhold. "Give us this day the needs of temporal life that we may the better progress toward eternal life," God might have taught. But God had given man the words he should pray and God knew, much better than did men, what the words signified. Certainly He intended to include freedom among man's needs—at least among the needs of those men who could not live unless they were free—for no man desires the things necessary to continue the miserable life of a slave. "Give us this day our freedom that we may adore Thee, the God of mercy." Within himself, Patrick felt his claim against God even more just than Erc's claim against Master Miliucc.

He drove the sheep a very short distance before he began his work of making bows and shafts. In three days he made one bow and assembled an arrow, then drove the arrow in singing flight into a distant tree. He had lost none of his skill during his six years in Ireland.

He was making a second bow when a deer emerged from a wood and walked slowly across the open land where the sheep grazed. Patrick fitted his arrow quickly into the completed bow—he would have deer meat for himself rather than the poor, dried fare provided by Master Miliucc.

He lowered the bow slowly, releasing the tension. He would not have deer meat, he decided. God had given him the opportunity of fasting—the food he might obtain with this weapon would be his "fast against God." He would content himself with the fare he had.

He worked steadily and rapidly, completing the shafts, testing them against tree trunks. In the fourth week, when he had fitted the last arrowhead to its shaft, he heard a voice while he slept, saying, "You have done well to fast. Soon you will go to your own country."

Patrick awakened, startled by the voice, enlivened by the promise. He knew he had not dreamed; he had heard the voice while he slept, but a voice of rich softness such as could not be heard in a dream.

During the week that followed, he waited expectantly but patiently. He led the sheep higher on the hills that they might crop the grass sweetened by winter's snows, but he also led them nearer to the village—and to the enclosure of Master Miliucc. On the seventh night, again he heard a voice saying to him, "Your ship is ready."

Through the first hours of the eighth day, Patrick puzzled at the meaning of the words. There could be no ship ready for him and Victoricus in this land of hills and forests and small streams. But in midmorning, a man appeared below in the glen, hallooing excitedly. He was indistinguishably small, but Patrick recognized the voice of Erc. He pushed the weapons under the projecting edge of a boulder, then hurried down the slope, leaving the sheep in the care of the dogs.

Erc was visibly excited, with an air of happy expectancy. He hurried through the customary words of greeting to tell the purpose of his mission. "You have an opportunity to escape, Patrick!" He watched Patrick's expression, then grasped his arms to emphasize his message. "You have an opportunity to escape! King Neal has been killed, and a battle is beginning to determine his successor."

Patrick regarded the smaller man uncomprehendingly. He was prepared for Erc's announcement, but he could not relate the death of Ireland's king, or selection of a new king, with escape.

Erc discerned Patrick's difficulty. "Sit down, Patrick."
He crouched down beside him, found a twig, and scratched
an oval on the ground. "This is Ireland," he explained. Rapidly he divided the oval into five equal parts. "This segment
at the top is Ulster; the next two below it are Meath and
Connaught. Ulster and Meath want one man to be king;
Connaught wants a different man. So a war is beginning
between Connaught on one side and Ulster and Meath on
the other."

Patrick tried to maintain his interest in Erc's explanation of the political situation and to understand the relation-
ship of this to his own situation.

Erc drew the twig to the left across the part he had designated as Ulster. "If you can make your way safely across
Ulster, then turn downward into Connaught, you will be
free. The people of Connaught will not capture and return
the slave of a lord of Ulster while they are warring against
Ulster."

Patrick leaned forward to study the outline drawn by
Erc. Now all was clear to him: The voice he had heard,
the death of Ireland's king, and escape were now joined
together. "Where are we now?"

Erc placed the twig high on the right side of the oval.
"We are here—in Ulster." He moved the twig downward
then to the left. "You must go in this direction to avoid
a large lake," he explained. "Circle around the bottom of
the lake and walk westward until you come to the sea."
He drew the twig to the left as he talked, until it touched
the edge of the oval, then moved it downward. "When you
come to the sea, walk south into Connaught." His expression became very serious. "Be alert as long as you are in
Ulster, Patrick."

Patrick stood up slowly. His whole being vibrated eagerly. "You'll need weapons, Patrick," Erc cautioned.

Patrick smiled broadly. "I have weapons, Erc—of the finest workmanship." He laughed at the wonder in Erc's countenance, then told him of Victoricus' labors. "But we shall need a tall ladder—sufficiently tall to reach the top of Master Miliucc's palisade."

Erc was stricken as he understood Patrick's purpose. "You must enter the enclosure?"

Patrick nodded and told of the night when Victoricus had boldly invaded the household of Master Miliucc for food and grease. "He risked his life that night for a youth he hardly knew—and saved my life. I won't abandon him."

Erc nodded soberly, aware of the added risk but agreeing that it was necessary for such a man as Victoricus. He grinned suddenly with his customary air of impudence. "You will have your ladder," he promised. "You will find it at the foot of the palisade on the side opposite the village— but it won't be there until after dark. When you finish with it, Patrick, put it in the wood at the foot of the hill below the enclosure." He stood for a moment, obviously reluctant to confront the moment of parting, then thrust out his hand. "I hope we never meet again," he said awkwardly.

Patrick grasped his hand. "May God remember your kindness, Erc."

Erc regarded him blankly. "God?" he repeated.

Patrick felt an intense regret. He had not sufficient time to explain his meaning—to tell this pagan friend of the God Who was so powerful and, at the same time, so generous to undeserving man. He would pray that God would arrange that Erc might know Him. "Someday you will understand," he assured.

He watched Erc descend the hill, wave from the glen at the bottom, and disappear. He walked up the slope to remain with the sheep and busy himself with the preparation of sufficient food for the beginning of the adventure. He gauged carefully the progress of the sun so that he could approach the enclosure under cover of darkness.

He found the ladder where Erc had promised. It scraped slightly as he raised it and he stood motionless and tense until sure that none had heard. He placed the weapons on the ground, climbed carefully and swung himself over the top of the palisade. He lowered his body, held momentarily by his fingers, then dropped to the ground. The motion reminded him of the boy—it was so long ago—who had enjoyed dropping from the wall of the hiberna at Bannaventa.

He moved confidently across the dark enclosure, found one of Master Miliucc's ladders, and returned to place it against the palisade. They could not risk the delay of carrying a ladder and lifting it into place together. He did not know where Victoricus would be sleeping—God must guide him—but would try first the place where the smith's helpers had slept in the past. He walked swiftly to the smithy, opened the door gently, and stepped inside.

A racking cough from the right destroyed the silence of the night even as it identified Victoricus. Patrick stood stiffly. The cough rattled in fierce spasms. In the darkness to the left, a man grumbled irritably; Patrick heard Victoricus struggle to a sitting position in an effort to relieve the affliction, then leave his sleeping place and approach the door. Patrick drew back carefully as Victoricus passed him, then followed after him.

Victoricus walked straight and purposefully from the building, coughing intermittently. He stopped and turned around as Patrick joined him. "I heard you come through the door," he whispered, then lapsed into another spasm.

Patrick grasped the older youth's arm—it was very thin and wasted—and guided him across the enclosure to the ladder. "You must stop coughing," he warned.

They stood together until Victoricus quieted. He touched Patrick's arm and started up the ladder. Patrick climbed closely behind him. When he told the incident years later in his *Confession,* he ignored his efforts in behalf of Victoricus and told only of himself: "Then I took to flight and left the man with whom I had stayed six years."

It was a slow flight in the beginning. They travelled little more than two miles during the night, then stopped for a day and night that Victoricus might rest. They advanced only a little over four miles on the second day and three on the third, but during the three days following, Victoricus enjoyed unusual strength and they moved a considerable distance southward; however, Patrick saw the fever flush mounting in the Roman's face and noted the increasing glossiness of his eyes. At the end of the sixth day, when they stopped to rest and eat on a low summit, Victoricus could not lie down because of the prolonged coughing that assailed him. He sat upright, resting against a great rock. "This is the end, Patrick," he gasped weakly.

Patrick tried to revive the spirit of pretense he had used since their escape, but the effort failed; he knew he had succeeded on other days only because Victoricus had pretended also. A heavy melancholy descended on him. "We will rest here several days," he decided.

Victoricus shook his head slightly. "Tonight is the end, Patrick—or perhaps tomorrow morning." He sat quietly for a time. "I never thought, when we first talked of escaping, that this would be the kind of escape God would give me. There were times, Patrick, when I thought God might let me escape so that I could return home, study, receive Holy Orders and return to these people."

Patrick watched Victoricus wonderingly. How could a man contemplate returning to this life from which they were escaping?

"I would think of Dichu and Eilethe and her sister," Victoricus continued. "I could never forget the day when Dichu told us he was afraid of that god of theirs."

"Cenn Cruaich?"

"Cenn Cruaich." Victoricus smiled weakly. "I felt so sorry for those children that I started forgetting to feel sorry for myself. I remembered how they listened to the story of the Nativity and dreamed how wonderful it would be to tell them how much that Infant loved them and all men."

The figures of Miliucc and Dann intruded into Patrick's mind but he did not interrupt Victoricus.

"Someone must do it, Patrick. Our Lord commanded the Apostles to 'make disciples of all nations. Go into the whole world and preach the gospel to every creature.'" His voice failed and he closed his eyes for a time. When he opened them again, he pulled himself slightly higher and leaned his head back so that he could look upward to the sky. "There are stars tonight—a beautiful night for going to God." He turned his head slightly to Patrick. "Keep the Faith," he whispered hoarsely. His body slumped sideways.

Patrick leaped to raise his fallen companion, but Victoricus lay limp in his arms.

6

THE loss of Victoricus weighted Patrick's steps; sorrow smothered the spirit of zest which had grown in him steadily since the beginning of the adventure. He knew he sorrowed for himself and because of his loss rather than because of the other's death, for the Roman had welcomed his escape; and the realization shortened the time of his own sorrow.

Faintly at first—so faintly that he did not know when it began—he became conscious of his freedom. The knowledge helped to counter sorrow. It gave new power to the thrust of his legs as he toiled across mountains, and added inches to his stride as he walked across level stretches of grass. He traveled rapidly, despite frequent detours to avoid villages, and became so intent on his progress that he nearly stumbled into the camp of a band of fighting men.

Whether they were men of Ulster or men of Connaught he could not know; but the incident alerted him to his recklessness. He had not escaped from Master Miliucc merely to escape and enjoy his freedom until recaptured by some other; he had escaped in order to escape Ireland itself and return to his father.

It was strange that a man could become so engrossed with an immediate purpose as almost—or even completely—to forget that he had another, more distant goal.

In the beginning, he had not been preoccupied with escape itself; his mind and imagination had been filled with memories of Bannaventa.

Time and difficulties had obscured memory. His attention had drawn away from the more distant goal of reunion with his father and concentrated on escape itself. Or perhaps Bannaventa had become meaningless when Victoricus told him that the Legion was no longer there but had been withdrawn to protect the borders of the Empire on the Continent—perhaps Rome itself.

His father? His father had probably suffered for a time, just as he had, from the sudden disruption of their lives. But, as time had healed his own wounds, so would it have healed his father's. He realized that the enforced separation, prolonged for so many years, had eradicated all sentimental affection for his father just as it had obscured reunion with his father as his distant goal; the finding of his father and being reunited with him had become an effect of escape rather than a motivating cause.

Spring was far advanced when Patrick finally came to the sea. "My ship was not near Master Miliucc's," he explained in his *Confession,* "but as far as two hundred miles away, in a country where I had never been and where I did not know a living soul. But I made my way, strengthened and protected and guided by God; and I feared nothing along the way." He turned south along the coast, as Erc had instructed, following the jagged mountain ridges that carried him safely past the fishing villages.

The day that marked the end of the eighth week of freedom was dull and overcast. Low, heavy clouds, dark and troubled, moved in from the sea. Strong gusts of wind tore at the trees, bending them in quick, graceful bows. At noon, when the sky had become very dark, a great rain curtain raced in from the sea.

Patrick found a small hut of interlaced boughs on a shelf exposed to the sea but secure against the rain and wind. The entrance faced to the south, overlooking a small cove with an inclined beach, cut into the base of the mountains. For a few minutes, he was able to look down on the towering waves that rushed into the cove; then the rain closed about the hut.

Not long after, the barking of dogs sounded clearly above the noise of the rain as it beat against the shelter and hissed downhill to the sea. Patrick tensed, ready to abandon the shelter to any who approached and seek safety in the blinding rain. The barking continued intermittently, and Patrick relaxed as he determined that the sound was not drawing closer.

The rain ceased in the last hours of the night. In the light of a troubled dawn, Patrick looked from his shelter on a world of drenched earth and fallen trees. Again he heard the barking of the dogs and looked down on the beach below the shelter.

A large boat lay on the sand, clear of the waters that had driven it from the sea. He could see three men straining against the prow, struggling to refloat it. In the middle of the vessel was a pen that enclosed a pack of restless wolfhounds.

Instantly Patrick understood the significance of the cargo. Only dogs intended for sale in France or Rome would be transported by sea; the boat was bound for the Continent.

He studied the three seamen carefully, satisfied himself that they were of ordinary strength and lightly armed, then hurried from his shelter. This was most certainly the boat designated by the voice that had said, "Your ship is ready."

The dogs barked more furiously, warning the seamen as he approached. They turned and drew their knives warily. The ship was still embedded where it had been.

Patrick slipped his bow from his shoulders, fitted an arrow into the thong and walked slowly toward the boat. "I seek passage," he called, but the men seemed not to understand. Patrick realized that the dogs overpowered the sound of his voice. "Quiet!" he shouted, lapsing into Latin. "Sit!" he commanded. The dogs obeyed the familiar sounds and Patrick repeated, "I seek passage."

The oldest of the three men answered him. "Seek elsewhere." He gestured toward the dogs now sitting in their penned area. "We have enough passengers." He raised his knife menacingly, threatening to throw it as Patrick moved closer. "Stay where you are—do not come nearer!" he shouted.

The loud voice excited the dogs and they resumed their barking so that again Patrick had first to quiet them. "I am peaceful," he addressed the leader.

"Only a slave and a Roman knows the words to command these dogs," the man retorted. He said something to the younger men in a low tone and the three drew apart.

"I am a Roman citizen," Patrick acknowledged. He saw that the three had separated so that at least two of their knives would strike him while he could strike only one of them with an arrow.

The leader raised his knife higher and the younger men held theirs ready. "Go away!" he growled. "By no means will we take you with us." His tone aroused the dogs and they began again their vicious barking.

Patrick backed away from the three, holding his weapon ready and prepared to dodge should any one or all three hurl their knives. When he had retreated a safe distance, he turned away from them and began to struggle up the incline to the ridge above the beach. He had not realized how high his hopes had soared; he knew it now by the intensity of disappointment that weighted his legs and drained his strength. He had not the will to turn south and continue his journey; he climbed toward the shelter.

Automatically, from habit born of lonely hours in the hills and valleys of Ulster, he began to pray. He asked nothing of God. Dejection numbed him against the very realization of need. He spoke—simply, trustfully—expelling disappointment by revealing it as any man does to a friend.

A shouting from the beach interrupted his prayer and he paused to look back. One of the three seamen was running across the sand towards the place where he had started to climb. "Come back, Roman! Come back! We will take you with us." In the boat behind the running figure, the dogs added their own clamor.

*   *   *   *   *

The distrust born of their initial encounter had carefully to be set aside. The captain, Aelred, pointed toward Patrick's weapons. "How shall we know you will not turn those against us and steal the dogs?"

"I will swear good faith by my God," Patrick offered.

"You are a Roman citizen and a Christian," Aelred reflected doubtfully.

"How shall I know," Patrick challenged, "that you will take me with you when I have helped you to refloat the ship?"

Aelred considered, then his face contorted into the semblance of a grin. "We will swear our good faith by Manannan mac Lir," he proposed.

Patrick puzzled at the answer. "Manannan mac Lir?"

"The god of the sea."

Patrick curled his tongue to spit disgustedly into the sand, but restrained the gesture. If he were to escape Ireland, he could not wait for a boat manned by Christians. "What work will I do on board?" he asked in token of acceptance.

Aelred measured Patrick's powerful frame. "You are strong. You can do as much as any of us."

Patrick put aside his lingering doubts. If he could not trust an oath sworn to a pagan god, he could rely upon the true God to protect him. He tossed his bow and his remaining arrows upward into the boat, then joined his strength to the others. They inched the boat slowly through the sand until it floated on the water of the cove.

They ran lightly before the wind that blew strongly in the wake of the storm. Great swells came upon them from the rear, lifted them gently, speeded them momentarily, then rolled ahead of them. The sky cleared and became a wide expanse of blue, touched by thin wisps of cloud. Aelred grasped the tiller bar, holding the ship to its course; there was no work for the other three in that sea and they lounged with the captain.

"Good wind! Good weather!" Aelred gloated. "You have brought good luck, Patrick."

Patrick moved his head in denial and smiled. "God is the author of all good, Aelred."

Aelred shrugged his shoulders. "Christians are satisfied with one God, Patrick. We Irish have many gods."

"You have one principal god," Patrick responded, "Cenn Cruaich."

Aelred grimaced ridiculously and the younger men laughed. "Cenn Cruaich is a god for landsmen, Patrick. A god of stone and metal. What good is such a god on the sea? He would sink and would sink us with him." Fair wind and good weather were improving his disposition.

Patrick laughed at Aelred's grotesque analysis.

"What is your God, Patrick? A God for landsmen or for seamen?"

Unbidden, the answer came readily to Patrick's tongue. "My God, Aelred"—he glanced toward the others to include them in his answer—"is the God who separated the land from the water, who rolled back the sea for His chosen people, who came to earth as a man and walked on the waves to prove that He is the God of land and sea and all else."

"Bah!" said Aelred. Then his curiosity surmounted his incredulity. "He walked on the waves?"

"Less than four hundred years ago." Patrick sensed their desire to know more of this strange event but sensed also the readiness of their hostility to a God opposed to their own. He let the conversation languish. The others would revive the subject.

The coast of Ireland glided by steadily. Patrick watched the rise and fall of the mountains, saw the edge of the land advance towards them, then fall away until it became very vague or, at times, even vanish from sight.

Restlessness of the dogs aroused him. He found food for them in a chest which Aelred indicated, then climbed over the pen surrounding the animals. Aelred called warningly and some of the dogs growled, but Patrick spoke softly and soothingly while they investigated him, their noses reaching easily to his chest.

"You're either very brave or very foolhardy," Aelred said doubtfully when Patrick climbed out of the pen.

Patrick laughed. "Dogs are my friends, Aelred." He dropped down to his place with the others. "And my God told man to rule the earth and subdue it—which gives man mastery over these animals."

Aelred pretended to be interested only in conversation to while away the time. "Tell us of this God Who walked on the waves, Patrick." He stretched as if to emphasize his lack of interest; his body swayed evenly with the movements of the boat.

Patrick told the story of Christ walking on the sea of Galilee and of Peter who also walked on the waves until his faith failed. He watched carefully the expressions of his three listeners. "I hoped they would come to the faith of Jesus Christ because they were pagans," he related later. He was prepared to discontinue the narration if they displayed hostility, but he saw evidence only of fascination and doubt.

"How do you know He walked on the water?" Aelred demanded. "The twelve who claimed they saw Him were His close friends."

"There were thousands on the shore that He left. They were surprised when they discovered that He had gone because the twelve had taken the only boats on that side of the sea. But those thousands suspected what He had done, so they hurried around the shore of the sea to find Him again. When they found Him, they knew certainly what He had done. There was no need for them to ask Him or the twelve."

All three were silent for some moments. Then one of the younger men went to the food chest, withdrew something, and threw it into the sea.

"What was that?" Patrick asked curiously. The seaman sat down without answering. Patrick glanced at Aelred.

"Honey," the captain explained tersely. "Honey to placate Manannan mac Lir."

Infrequently, during the two days that followed, one or another asked some question that permitted Patrick to tell them more about God. The continuing good wind and weather, tangible assurance of Manannan mac Lir's abiding good humor, encouraged their curiosity, though several times each day they cast more honey into the sea.

"After three days we reached land," Patrick recounted the end of the voyage. With favoring wind and tide they drove in toward a broad, deep beach, backed by stunted trees that struggled for life in the sandy loam. Directly before the boat were the charred outlines of burned buildings, probably a fishing village. Patrick turned to Aelred and pointed to the blackened area.

Aelred was looking intently at the ruined settlement, his expression grave and troubled. He seemed to understand Patrick's unspoken question. "A year ago," he said thoughtfully, "forty people lived there."

Patrick examined the beach in each direction. "They might have moved," he said without conviction.

Aelred shook his head. "If their village burned, they would have built another beside it."

They beached the boat and plodded across the sand, still warm from the heat of the sun, to the site of the village at the edge of the trees. Aelred stopped them and pointed to two charred bodies almost indistinguishable from the burned wood. "Old people," he said calmly, as though he had found precisely what he expected to find.

One of the dogs barked from the boat, then another, then all together, resentful of being abandoned. Aelred turned quickly. "Quiet them, Patrick!"

Patrick responded automatically to the urgent tone of the order. He ran back to the boat, shouting as he did, to end the noise. Obediently the dogs sat, contented with his presence. Aelred and the seamen followed.

Aelred gestured in the direction of the village. "Raiders did that—we don't know how long ago. Two weeks, three, four. They may be a hundred miles away—or only five. If they find us, they will take us with the young people they took from the village."

"Put back to sea," Patrick proposed.

"Without food or water?" Momentarily Aelred lapsed into the seaman's contempt for a landsman's ignorance. "You had better pray to your God, Patrick," he muttered, "and keep the dogs quiet," he added harshly. His bad humor evaporated as quickly as it had arisen. "Raiders know that where there are dogs, there are humans," he grumbled.

Patrick recovered his bow and few remaining arrows from the place where he had stored them during the voyage—he had not won his freedom from the Irish to become a slave to unknown others. He became aware, suddenly, that the others were watching him; already alarmed by the evidence of enemies, they were distrustful of him also because he was armed. He slipped the bow over his head so that it hung loosely from his shoulder before he turned to rejoin them.

Aelred seemed satisfied with the gesture. "We will sleep tonight among those trees behind the beach," he decided. "We will start inland tomorrow."

"For twenty-eight days we travelled through a desert," was Patrick's method of describing the journey across France. They held their course close to the Roman military road and came regularly upon the sites of other villages, all burned as the first, with bodies scattered amid the ruins. In the very first of those days, they knew that they were seeing the work, not of a small band of raiders, but of an entire army that had devastated the country through which it passed.

Even wild animals had vanished before the advance of the unknown, savage army. On the first two days, in the country nearest to the sea, Patrick killed two deer with his arrows, enabling both men and dogs to eat their fill. In following days, he could find only hares, but so few that the men ate the flesh and gave the hides and entrails to the dogs. In the second week, he proposed that the dogs be released from their leashes and be permitted to forage for themselves.

Aelred shook his head immediately in refusal. "Those dogs cost us everything we owned. They will stay with us," he said firmly. He looked to the two younger men, and both nodded their agreement.

"They needn't cost you your life," Patrick retorted emphatically. "I can find hardly enough food for the four of us."

"The dogs remain with us," Aelred repeated stubbornly.

Day by day, their progress slowed; a field of wild berries sufficed to stop the march completely while the men ate, but the dogs sank to the ground. Each day, Patrick returned from the hunt with a lesser number of hares. Dogs and men grew gaunt and weak. The dogs became dispiritedly quiet while the four men became more sullen; even the three Irish fell into bitter dispute about some insignificant matter until Patrick put an end to their bickering. Again and again, Patrick urged release of the dogs. "If you insist on holding them," he insisted one night, "we will either eat them or be eaten by them."

Aelred reacted furiously to the gruesome thought. "Where is that great, good God of yours?" he demanded bitterly. "He walked on the water, He fed thousands with a few loaves and fishes—or so you told us," he said sarcastically. "You say that your God is great and all-powerful? Why, then, do you not pray that He give us food?" He spat to demonstrate his contempt. "Tell Him to let us see Him, because we cannot hope ever to see another human."

Patrick's whole being recoiled from the blasphemous words. The muscles of his body contracted with a rage that demanded he leap and kill the presumptuous man who spoke so boldly against God. Then the very intensity of his anger defeated itself. It was a rage so tremendous that its greatness shocked him. Why was he so maddened? Other men had said much the same words to Christ while He hung on the Cross. Christ had not killed them. His body relaxed. His anger would not convince these three; only God Himself could do that.

"Believe in my God," he pleaded suddenly. "Believe that my God is the Lord of all, that He is good, that He does all things according to His wisdom. Believe in Him, believe that nothing is impossible to Him so that He can put food in our way." None of them answered him. He looked at each in turn, but they would not look at him.

Through most of the night hours Patrick prayed. At times, fatigue overpowered him, and he slept for a time. Repeatedly he roused himself and resumed his prayers confidently. With dawn the others awakened, and Patrick moved to precede them as was their custom.

A sound from the woods startled him. He stopped and raised his hand warningly to stop the others. More noises sounded from the woods—the scraping of feet on the earth and the unmistakable grunting of pigs. Then, singly and in pairs and threes, thirty pigs marched from the woods into the road.

The astonishing answer to his night of prayer stunned Patrick. He stood transfixed, watching the animals. Behind him, one of the men shouted suddenly, and all three leaped forward with their knives to seize the food put in their way.

*   *   *   *   *

"We stopped in that place two days and nights," Patrick recorded, "and recovered our strength completely. We gave the hounds their fill so that they regained their liveliness of body and spirit."

The discord that had intruded among the four as a consequence of starvation and danger gave way to renewed camaraderie. Food and revival of physical strength lifted their hopes; they regarded the future optimistically. Aelred and his two companions, their spirits restored by their good fortune, became friendly once more to each other and to Patrick.

Willingly Patrick joined in the laughter and bantering of the others. Frequently, his mind returned to the marvel of the food placed in their path after his night of prayer, but it turned readily from contemplation to jesting with the others. Several times he thought to remind them of his plea that they believe in the providence of God; but the pleasure of companionship dissuaded him from introducing new cause for dispute.

He was distracted also by anticipation of the end of the journey, for Aelred reckoned that they were very near the Mediterranean Sea and could hope to find another boat that would carry them across the water to Rome. He assured himself that he would have ample time and opportunity, during that voyage, for impressing on these pagans a knowledge and awareness of the goodness of God.

On the second night, however, he later recalled: "While I was asleep, Satan assailed me violently—an attack I shall never forget. He fell upon me with overwhelming power; it was as though a huge boulder pinioned me to the ground, for I could not move a muscle. My helplessness increased my terror. But God did not abandon me, for He put into my mind to see, as a symbol, the sun rising in the sky of my night and to shout, 'Savior! Savior!' As I shouted with all my might, suddenly the splendor of the sun fell upon me; I felt Satan thrown from me. I believe that I was delivered by Christ, my Lord, and that His Spirit, even then, was crying out in my behalf."

Patrick awakened, wet with perspiration from his terror and his efforts to struggle against the dread power that had held him. He lay looking up through the trees at the stars, trying to understand the experience. He could not return to sleep; when dawn brightened the sky, he was first to arise in readiness for resumption of their journey.

He moved ahead of the others, alert for signs or sounds of game. He had gone a very short distance when the shout of one of the others caused him to turn. One of the younger men was standing by a tree beckoning to his two companions. They drew something from within the tree trunk, talking seriously together for a moment, then ate of whatever they had found. One motioned toward Patrick and he retraced his steps to join them.

"Honey, Patrick," Aelred explained, his hands dripping the thin liquid. He stepped back a pace and motioned toward the tree. "Eat," he offered.

Patrick moved toward the tree, then felt a strange reluctance.

One of the younger men glanced at him curiously. "Eat," he urged. "We are offering this as a sacrifice to Cenn Cruaich, the land god, for the pigs he put before us."

Patrick drew back from the sweet food that had suddenly become loathsome and revolting. "I want none," he said. He turned quickly and walked again along the road.

He knew now the meaning of the night's experience, when Satan assailed him. He had permitted himself to feast and rejoice with his pagan companions for two full days while neglecting to solicit their gratitude to the one true God Who had granted them this boon. So the three pagans, having found the wild honey, symbolic food of the heathen god, had attributed to Cenn Cruaich what had been given them by the God of all.

He realized that Satan had seen his sloth and had thought to consolidate his victory by attacking and terrorizing him in the night and completely subjugating him. Only the intervention of God had saved him.

A shameful knowledge of his faithlessness burdened Patrick through that day. At the night meal, when they ate of the animals he had hunted, he endeavored to remedy his indolence by speaking of God, of God's bounty, and of the night when he had pleaded with them to believe in God. The three were uninterested. They were strong and well fed; they felt no need of God.

Through each of ten nights, Patrick continued his efforts, pressing them to remember that they had traveled twenty-eight days with little food until they had nearly starved, that God suddenly had granted them an abundance of food, that God had continued to bless them with abundant food each day since. On the first few of these nights, the three listened patiently but, as he continued his efforts, they laughed irreverently. On the tenth night, Aelred told Patrick curtly they would hear no more.

During those days, men and dogs advanced rapidly through country that had escaped plundering but was devoid of human life. They came regularly upon villages where the buildings were intact, but without people or livestock, except for pigs roaming freely in the adjacent country or a few sheep grazing peacefully. The people seemed to have learned of the raiders and abandoned their homes, taking with them only those animals they could gather quickly together. The raiders had pursued them, and so rapidly that they had not delayed to ravage the country. When the four, with the dogs, came to the sea, they discovered that all boats had disappeared; they were forced to continue along the land route.

On the morning after Aelred had curtly forbidden Patrick to continue his pleas and sermons, they advanced through a country of low hills, Patrick preceding the others. He came to a place where the road was confined by brush-covered slopes on either side, when a horde of men burst from the bushes and fell upon him. He had not time to unsling his bow nor even to draw his knife; he could do nothing more than utter a single shout of warning to the three following him before he was crushed to the ground.

His first impression was that he had been recaptured by another band of Irish raiders until one of the group, apparently their leader, spoke commandingly to the others in a tongue completely unlike the Irish. He realized, too, that these men did not wear the accustomed battle dress of the Irish; instead of battle horns, they wore heads of wild animals as a kind of helmet and, instead of the simple leather shield, had both shield and breastplate of iron.

Many of the attackers separated obediently from the group and, yelling hideously, ran toward Aelred and his partners. Patrick heard the shouting of the Irish mingled with the strange shouts of the enemy, heard the snarling of the dogs leaping instinctively to assist their masters, heard the struggle. The tumult stopped as his captors stood up and gestured for him to stand. Two of the six who had remained with him grasped his arms, and the group hurried back along the road to the place where their companions stood.

Two of the enemy lay dead in the road; but, beside them and dead also, lay Aelred and his partners. Nearby were the bodies of the dogs, pierced and bludgeoned.

Patrick looked down sadly on the three Irish. If only God had permitted them to live a little longer, perhaps he might have brought them to the faith of Jesus Christ.

7

PATRICK'S sorrow gave way to despondency. He had endured so much, he had travelled so far, he knew the little distance remaining before achieving his goal. One of his captors shoved him roughly to indicate the direction he should go, and he obeyed without resisting.

Six of the men accompanied him. They were big men with long yellow manes that fell grotesquely from beneath the animal's heads they used as helmets. They were bigger and more powerful than most of the Irish he had seen.

He heard the sounds of the camp while they were yet some distance from it—a babble of loud, raucous sounds of many people. It was a big camp of wagons and tents placed haphazardly in the long valley. From the hill above it, Patrick saw women and children gathered into family groups before each tent. Some of the children ran toward the group to welcome the six and jeer their prisoner; the women screamed greetings as the group passed through the camp to a place where other captives, men and women, sat listlessly on the ground.

One of the guards pointed to the ground, and Patrick began to sit down; his action was too slow and the savage suddenly kicked his feet from beneath him so that he fell to the ground. The fall shocked him—freed him from the despondency pressing against him. He leaped to his feet,

smashed powerfully at his tormentor's face and struck a
second blow at the next guard before he was overwhelmed
and borne to the ground under the combined weight of the
others.

They did him no other harm except to tie his hands
behind him; they spoke laughingly to each other as they
worked, as though they had enjoyed the incident. The two
whom Patrick had struck down regained their feet and
approached threateningly, but the others took them away
before they could retaliate.

"Are you a Christian?" a man beside him asked.

Patrick glanced at the other—a round-faced man, a year
or two older than himself but very stout as though accustomed to a soft manner of life. He nodded without interest,
then looked about at the dispirited captives and the guards
watching them. He felt some satisfaction as he discovered that two guards stood directly behind him, despite his
helplessness.

"Where are you from?" his companion asked.

Patrick turned the question about in his mind. Where
was he from? Was he from Britain? Was he a Roman citizen? Or was he merely a slave recently escaped from Ireland to be re-enslaved by these new captors? "Britain," he
said shortly.

"Britain? Then you would not know. You needn't fight;
here in France and Italy, the Christians collect money regularly and use it to ransom Christians who are taken captive by these tribesmen. We will be ransomed," he added
encouragingly.

The man's softness annoyed Patrick. "I escaped from
slavery in Ireland only three months ago," he said harshly.
"I was a slave for six years, but no one ransomed me or

other Christians enslaved there." He looked at the other disagreeably.

The man's cheerfulness faded. "The Christians here will ransom us," he affirmed, trying to regain his spirit of conviction.

"Who are these tribesmen?" Patrick asked.

"Suevi, a tribe from across the Rhine. They often take prisoners so that they will receive ransom for them." He continued struggling to restore his confidence.

Patrick said nothing more. For a time, his companion attempted to continue the conversation, but Patrick did not listen to him. He counted the captives—seventeen men and twenty-one women, all young—with eight tribesmen guarding them. They seemed to be on the edge of the camp, midway along its length. If he could free his hands during the night . . .

At midday, the guards roused some of the men, sending a group to bring water, two others to bring a great iron pot, more to bring meat and wood. Those chosen went willingly and knowingly about their tasks as though already accustomed and resigned to this life. Other captives who had been working about the camp joined the group.

Patrick's hope stirred as he counted the total. The prisoners numbered at least sixty—enough that, when all were together at night, the guards would be less attentive to one individual among them. A guard released his hands that he might eat, muttering warningly as he did. Patrick nodded resignedly but with sufficient convincingness that he was not bound again after he had eaten.

The day passed slowly; the ritual of wood, water and meat was repeated in late afternoon. Darkness at long last cloaked the ugliness of earth; the camp quieted.

The fire, built to cook the food and fueled lightly to ward away the chill of the night, cast a soft, uncertain light over the captives. By that light, Patrick watched a young tribesman make his way through the prisoners as though searching among them. He bent down suddenly, reaching toward one hidden in the shadows. The captive screamed— the frightened scream of a young woman—as the tribesman pulled her to her feet. Other women cried out and some men mumbled fearfully.

Patrick leaned forward, his muscles tensing. The girl fought against the tribesman, kicking at him and struggling to free herself; her screams mounted higher as she realized her weakness and the man's strength. Patrick leaped from his place, then fell prostrate under the blow of a guard who had anticipated him. He tried to rise but the guard was upon him instantly, gouging both knees into his back. A spasm of pain forced him to remain flat on the ground.

The girl's screams stopped abruptly. Patrick saw that she had wrested one hand free and snatched the tribesman's knife from his belt. The knife flashed in the light of the fire as she raised it and plunged it into her breast.

The guard who had struck him and held him to the ground lifted his weight slowly and deliberately as though even his savage nature was shocked by the scene. He backed away into the shadows as Patrick regained his feet.

On the other side of the fire, men and women clustered around the fallen girl. Patrick watched contemptuously while they aided in death the one all of them had feared to aid in life. He moved again to the place where he had crouched, leaned back against a rock and watched the group on the other side of the fire carry the lifeless body into the far shadows where the light did not penetrate.

He understood their timidity. They expected to be ransomed, as did the soft young man, and wished to live until
they were. They would cherish life as long as they retained
that hope of being ransomed.

Perhaps the girl had also cherished life until human brutality revealed vividly that mortal life is not sufficient com-
pensation for loss of human dignity. In a single moment,
she had confronted the degradation of slavery and escaped
from it by the one means available to her. Now she was free.

He would also be free! A guard might intercept him but
he would be free! He would be free either with the freedom
he had won when he escaped from Master Miliucc's or he
would be free with the freedom the unknown girl had won.
He drew up his knees and lowered his head, pretending to
sleep. He prayed.

Slowly, almost imperceptibly, he let his body lean forward. He let one hand drop to his side and rest loosely on
the ground so that he could spring up quickly, wheel about
and race into the darkness—to freedom.

"You will be with them two months," a voice said
clearly.

Patrick sat very still, his body tensed for escape, his
attention arrested by the unexpected announcement. He
knew that voice. It was the voice that once had said to him,
"You have done well to fast. Soon you will go to your own
country." It was the same voice that, at another time, had
told, "Your ship is ready." He knew that voice.

He would be with his captors two months? His nature
rebelled against the prophecy. He would remain two months
to be struck and kicked? enslaved by these savages? to witness more scenes such as he had this night? Angry resentment mounted against such a life.

He sat stiffly, held between two powerful forces. He was free to decide between the two, free to accept the grace of God by which man does whatever God orders, or free to reject that grace and pursue his own desires. No force could prevent him from saying he would not stay two months with his captors—nor yet two minutes.

He could continue the purpose for which he was now tensely prepared. He could leap from his place, dash into the darkness and win either freedom from his captors or freedom from life itself.

Perhaps it was not the voice—he tried to doubt that he had indeed heard the same voice. He could doubt, he knew—he could convince himself. He could doubt by deliberately deceiving himself. But only cowards deceive themselves and he was not a coward. He had never been a coward; he did not want now to make himself into one. The voice was genuine. He could not rest his decision on a pretense.

Yet the voice was not the same as it had seemed on those earlier occasions. In the past, it was warm, comforting, inspiring. Now it seemed to scold as though imposing a penalty against him rather than promising delivery from his captors at a future time.

The announced period of two months emphasized that it was a penalty as well as a promise. He knew the significance of "two months." He remembered some of his fellow slaves in Master Miliucc's establishment—slaves who had failed to perform a task given them—who had been punished by reduction of their food allotment for a period of two months.

The realization made more difficult acceptance of the penalty imposed on him. To relax and remain where he was, to submit to this sentence, demanded admission that he had failed to perform a task assigned to him. He did not want to confront his dereliction, did not want to gaze on his weaknesses and faults; he wished to see himself as he wished others to see him.

That, too, was cowardice, he admitted. To flee from the sight of ugliness in one's soul is as great—or even greater cowardice—as to flee from a mortal enemy.

Deliberately he permitted memory to convey him backward to the beginning of the day. He stood again, as he had that morning, looking down on the bodies of the two dead tribesmen and the bodies of Aelred and his younger partners.

His attention diverted readily and eagerly to the group who now returned after disposing of the girl's body. He forced it to return again to the study of his actions of the day.

He had rested and feasted with Aelred, after the long period of starvation—with the three whom he had hoped "would come to the faith of Jesus Christ." They had not come to that faith in life; now they lay dead beneath a cairn of stones, deprived eternally of the knowledge and love of their Creator.

He had not deprived them of that faith! He had pleaded with them to believe firmly in his God on the night before the pigs walked into the road. And every night of the ten that had passed since they had found the wild honey, he had talked to them of God and His Divine Son. Only last night, Aelred had ended his efforts by his curt dismissal of the matter. That they died without having received the faith of Jesus Christ was of their own doing, not of his.

He could not deceive himself. The three had indeed

resisted him before food was placed in their path and again after they had rested two days and regained their strength. But they had not resisted him during those two days: He had said nothing in those days to incite resistance. They might have resisted, had he spoken; they might have gone to their deaths, still pagan, as they did this day.

What the three might have done could not obscure the increasing knowledge of his guilt. He had rested and feasted with them and had let pass the opportunity of impressing upon them their indebtedness to God, who had provided for them so mercifully. He had rested and feasted as a pagan himself while the memory of their ordeal faded. He had neglected the task assigned him until, refreshed and strengthened, the three felt no need of God.

Even this day he had repeated the basic fault of forgetting God. He had permitted himself to submit to despondency, then veered suddenly to rash determination to escape or die. So soon had he forgotten that, as God had permitted him to be enslaved by the Irish that he might be brought to the knowledge of God, so God must also have permitted him to be captured by these Suevi for his own good.

Steadily, without faltering, without wavering, Patrick contemplated his guilt. He let his body relax and settle backward. He would not resist. He would accept willingly the punishment imposed by God; he would remain "with them two months."

*   *   *   *   *

Steadfastly Patrick endured the allotted time of punishment. On the morning of the second day, he was taken with other captives and put with four slaves, strong as himself, who were water-bearers for the camp of the Suevi. Under the watchful eyes of a guard, he filed after the others to a stream, filled two pigskins which had been cured and sewed for the purpose, fastened each to the ends of a yoke, and began a steady round of numbing labor. One bearer who attempted to carry only partially filled skins drew curses and blows from the guard as a lesson to the others. When the camp moved, after each two or three days, the five were given the heaviest burdens to carry.

At night, they were not returned to the main group of prisoners but held apart, on the edge of the camp nearest the stream so that they could resume their labor with the first light of dawn. That had its compensations, Patrick appreciated, remembering the sight he had witnessed on the first night and his vain effort to help another. They spoke very little; their labor deprived them of both the spirit and strength to speak. At night, they slept as dead men.

Patrick became accustomed to the ordeal, his spirits sustained by the certainty of release, encouraged also by the steady southeastward movement of the tribe toward Rome. He was being delayed, he assured himself, but was moving toward his goal.

He counted the days. On the fifty-eighth, the tribe moved across a mountain ridge, and from that height he glimpsed the shimmering whiteness of the Eternal City. His expectations mounted steadily that day and the next.

The sixtieth day was no different from the fifty-nine that had preceded it, except that the tribe moved once again; Patrick knew that they must have drawn very close to the walls of Rome. He labored under the burden imposed on him, alert to every incident of the day, but saw no opportunity of escape from the vigilant guard. At nightfall, he lay down wearily to struggle against doubt and despair. He slept.

A shout of alarm sounded from the farther side of the camp. A second followed from another point. Suevi tribesmen plunged from their tents into the light of their fires. Other alarms sounded from many places along the edges of the camp, certain indication that an enemy surrounded it.

The guard grunted an order excitedly and motioned the five to move toward the center of the camp. Patrick stood up obediently to obey the order. His hopes soared. Behind him in the darkness beyond the edge of the camp, he heard a noise as of a man falling over some unseen obstacle; the guard also heard, turned about, and moved toward the sound. Patrick glanced backward and saw tiny flashes— the reflections of firelight on the polished armor of Roman legionnaires! The four other bearers ran fearfully from the scene toward the center of the camp; Patrick dropped to the ground and lay still.

Men rushed past; some stumbled over the prostrate form, then continued on their way. Shouting and screaming filled the night. Patrick raised his head and saw legionnaires methodically cutting down tribesmen with their women and children, and hurling brands from the fires on to the Suevi tents. Close to him, a young man wearing the epaulets of a centurion directed his legionnaires.

"I am a Roman citizen!" Patrick shouted.

The Centurion swung around and moved toward him, holding his sword high. "Stand!" he ordered.

Patrick obeyed eagerly, holding his arms stretched in front of him and turning his back to the officer as legionnaires required of their prisoners. A great joy surged through him; his term of punishment had ended. "So it came to pass," he told in his *Confession,* "on the sixtieth night, the Lord delivered me out of the hands of my captors."

Behind him, Patrick heard the Centurion order two men from the fighting. The two searched him then grasped his arms and guided him along the moonlit path they had trampled on their approach. They came to a road, and the guides turned Patrick to the right. Behind them, from the Suevi camp, a bugle blared.

"They are withdrawing!" Patrick exclaimed. "There are more than sixty Christians held there."

"We are not an army," one of the guides muttered. "There are hardly more than sixty men in this command."

"The camp was surrounded," Patrick argued.

Both men laughed. "It was surrounded by decoys," one answered, "to draw the main strength of those barbarians away from the section we raided."

Other legionnaires appeared behind them and formed into a column as they marched. Patrick glanced back— the number of men certainly was much smaller than he expected and certainly fewer than the tribesmen of the Suevi. This was not an expedition sent to attack and exterminate the savages, he realized; it was nothing more than a patrol that had discovered the tribesmen, distracted them by many feints, then fallen on one small section to do as much damage as possible.

And he had been in that one section! The realization startled him. God had promised that his punishment would continue sixty days; the legionnaires had delivered him, and only him, and without effort by him, on the sixtieth day.

The Centurion appeared and took his place at the head of the column. He motioned for Patrick to walk beside him. "Your name and home?" he questioned.

"Patrick from Britain. I am the son of Calpornius, a decurion of the Twentieth Legion."

The Centurion turned his head and examined Patrick suspiciously. "The Twentieth is not in Britain," he contradicted.

"I know," Patrick agreed. "I was taken from Britain by Irish raiders and held as a slave for six years. There I learned that the Twentieth had been recalled to Rome—I learned about that," he digressed, "from a Roman named Victoricus. Did you know him?"

The explanation, probably supported by Patrick's ragged clothing and unkemptness, countered the officer's initial suspicion. "Victoricus is a common name."

"The son of Pinianus," Patrick added.

The Centurion considered the answer while he watched alertly the road before them and the fields on either side. "Did this Victoricus describe his father, tell his occupation and the like?"

"He said that he resembled his father—so his father should be tall though not as tall as I am, and slender." Patrick continued to describe Victoricus minutely. "I don't remember that he ever told his father's occupation. He did say that his father was nearly forty when he married, so he should be sixty-five or more now."

"His mother?" the Centurion asked.

"Lady Melania. But she died when Victoricus was about twelve." He waited for other questions, but the Centurion seemed satisfied. "You did not know him?" he observed questioningly.

"I knew him," the Centurion admitted. "We were very good friends. From the way you have referred to him," he continued tonelessly, "he is dead."

Patrick noted the depressed tone as if the man had lost many friends to death. "He died," he said simply. "We escaped together from the man who owned us, but he died before we could escape from Ireland. I built a cairn over him."

The Centurion offered no comment. Patrick thought of many questions he wanted to ask, but the Roman's manner discouraged him. The weapons of the men in the column behind them sounded a dirge in rhythm with the even pacing of their march.

The road climbed slightly for a short distance; from the crest of the hill, Patrick saw the wall of the city and, beyond it, gleaming softly in the moonlight, the white buildings. "Rome!" he breathed.

The single word recalled the Centurion's attention. "I had intended taking you to the authorities for questioning," he commented in a more friendly manner. "Instead, I shall take you directly to Senator Pinianus so you can tell him about Victoricus."

"Senator? Victoricus never referred to his father as a Senator," Patrick objected.

A touch of humor appeared in the Roman's voice. "That would be like him. If you were with him in Ireland for six years," he added, "the Senator will want you to stay with him and tell him all that you can remember. Victoricus was the Senator's only child."

Patrick considered the arrangement uneasily. "I thought I might find my father as soon as I arrived in Rome and stay with him. I could visit the Senator," he proposed.

The Centurion shook his head regretfully. "I'm sorry. I forgot your purpose," he apologized. "But your father will not be in Rome. The Twentieth was sent to the north with other legions to drive back the Goths—at least to delay them," he amended darkly.

Patrick felt pain as great as any he had suffered from physical blows. He looked at the great bulk of the city he had thought would be the end of his journey. It was not the end. Not the end? He must continue further? Must go on, wandering endlessly over the face of the earth?

"You can't attempt to go north," the Centurion said as if he discerned Patrick's thoughts. "The country is full of raiders like those you were with tonight. You must stay in Rome until the country has been cleared or the Twentieth returns. And, since you must stay," he said encouragingly, "you would do well to stay with the Senator."

They halted briefly at the gates while the Centurion and the sentries exchanged a series of signs and countersigns. When the sentries opened the gates and admitted the column into the city, the Centurion gave over his command to a subordinate and guided Patrick to the left into a way that rose evenly up the side of a hill. "This is the Viminal," he explained. "The Senator's home is on the top."

Patrick looked up at the crest. He could see the cone-shaped tops of poplars silhouetted against the sky. Even as he looked, he experienced a strange inner sensation, as if something or someone were prodding the interior senses. Memory responded to the goad, then understanding followed: He was disappointed that he was approaching Senator Pinianus, rather than his own father, because he was more aware of his own purpose than of God's will.

Five months had elapsed since the night when he and Victoricus had fled Master Miliucc's establishment. In those five months, he had thought of his escape only as a boon—a great boon—granted by God in answer to his prayers. That was not so—he had prayed not only to escape but also to be reunited with his father. Had God granted escape entirely because of his prayers, He would not have subjected him to the hardships of crossing France with Aelred and the other two Irish, would not have permitted him to be captured by the Suevi; rather would God, having granted escape from Ireland, have speeded him to a full realization of his goal and reunion with his father.

He knew—he had long known—that God had permitted him to be enslaved by the Irish in order that he would learn to know and love his Heavenly Father. Now understanding arranged all the events of the six and one half years and clarified their significance. God had permitted him to escape from Ireland when the term of enslavement had gained His purpose. God had permitted him to be captured by the Suevi, not only to punish him, but also to impress upon him a constant awareness of God's presence, His power, His providence. God willed or permitted that he would come to Rome seeking his father and be disappointed; from disappointment he would understand that although he pursued his goal of his own will, he was moved by the will of God.

To what end? Something relating to Senator Pinianus? to Rome? or to himself? He dismissed conjecture. It sufficed that he be ever mindful of God and hold himself alert to His will.

8

GOD'S purpose, as revealed by events during the
months following the arrival of Patrick at the home
of Senator Pinianus, seemed to be directed exclusively
to Patrick's physical well-being. It were as though God
desired that Patrick rest and recover from the physical
hardships he had suffered during the seven years since he
had been taken captive, that he enjoy the pleasures of life
which had been denied him, that he relax in the security of
Rome's impregnable walls, that he be diverted by the mag-
nificence of the Eternal City and refreshed by the civilized
peoples crowding the streets, that he know again the luxury
of cleanliness of body and soft, fine linens.

In the establishment atop the Viminal Hill—which Senator Pinianus termed a villa but which Patrick, remembering his father's little villa at Bannaventa, could regard only
as a palace—he was a son rather than a guest or, even, an
honored guest. He had for himself the great room that had
once been Victoricus', slept on the couch which his friend
had used, walked through a high and wide doorway that
opened from his room on to the formal terrace, and looked
down from the heights of the terrace on the city which was
the heart and mind and soul of the civilized world.

Victoricus had told him of this life while they lay in
the darkness of the stable at Master Miliucc's. He had

listened, fascinated by the description of a world that was illusory and unreal—sometimes he had thought that Victoricus exaggerated, deceived by his memory. His friend had not exaggerated; rather had he minimized and deprecated. Perhaps he had been unable to describe accurately life in this city that dominated the world. Neither had Victoricus conveyed accurately the position of his father in the affairs of the city; for the great men of Rome came daily to consult with the Senator, and both men and their ladies came eagerly to enjoy the dinners and music of the great house.

The gatherings made Patrick sensitive to his deficiencies, and especially so when the Senator's two nephews appeared with their wives, for these four exaggerated their greetings to Patrick with the obvious purpose of increasing his discomfort. He knew the handsomeness of his appearance in the Roman clothing that accentuated his height, his depth of chest and strength; but he was painfully conscious of his deficiencies in those qualities which are not bestowed by nature but obtained by effort—deficiencies which, later, he would describe as "rusticity." In the company of well-spoken men and gentle women, he remained close to his dignified, gracious host, lest some guest, unaware of his fumbling speech and rusticity of manners, should engage him in conversation without the support of Senator Pinianus. Remembering those days many years later he wrote, "I know perfectly well that poverty and misfortune become me better than riches and pleasures."

With Senator Pinianus, his ease and confidence revived, for the father of Victoricus was as tolerant as the son who had resembled him. Once Patrick expressed regret that he was not more accomplished in social graces.

The Senator dismissed the matter lightly. "They are acquired in time, Patrick." He smiled. "I've noticed that when we eat, you look about and do as I and the others do; that is the first and principal rule of all social conduct. Later, you will observe how others speak, will note the subjects that claim their attention and will imitate them in that also. As to other matters, Patrick, do not be anxious to imitate; hold firmly to your own principles."

Patrick did not understand his patron's allusion to "other matters."

"You've heard these people discuss religious matters," Senator Pinianus prompted.

Patrick nodded hesitantly. "I heard some say that our salvation begins when we ask God for the grace to begin it. I could not agree with them."

"What did you say?"

Patrick shook his head quickly. "I said nothing. I am not learned as they are."

"What would you have said?"

Patrick averted his eyes uncomfortably. "I would have said that the priest in the church at the foot of the hill preaches that God must give us grace, of His bounty, before we can so much as desire salvation."

His host nodded encouragingly.

"I would have said that, before I was carried to Ireland as a slave, I was like a stone lying in the deep mire; but there God came in His mercy and power, lifted me up, raised me and placed me atop a high wall. I had never the desire to know Him before that and would never have had the desire except that He came and gave me the grace to desire knowledge of Him."

"Excellent, Patrick," Senator Pinianus approved.

He laughed delightedly. "Deep mire and a high wall," he repeated. "You express the same thought as Bishop Augustine but much more vividly. Keep that talent, Patrick."

Patrick seized eagerly the opportunity to divert the conversation from himself. "I have heard some speak of him."

"Favorably or unfavorably?"

"Both," Patrick answered. "Who is he?"

Senator Pinianus seemed about to explain, then decided against it. "I will let you learn to know him yourself, Patrick." He left the room but soon returned carrying a thick volume of bound manuscript. "Augustine is Bishop of Hippo on the farther side of the Mediterranean. He wrote this to tell all the world of God's great mercy toward him and to all men. Some are willing to accept his evaluation of human nature, others are not. Read it."

Patrick began reluctantly the arduous task of reading; but, what he began only to please his patron, he continued in order to satisfy his own wonderment. This Bishop Augustine both knew of God's mercy and could tell others of that mercy. When Senator Pinianus asked him, after several weeks, of his progress, Patrick shook his head regretfully. "I wish I had esteemed education more during my school days; the difficulty of reading interferes with my pleasure."

Through the months of indolent, pleasurable life, while Patrick read Bishop Augustine's *Confessions* and Romans waited fearfully for news of battle in the north, Patrick did not forget the great preeminent question of God's purpose. He went early each morning to attend the Mass celebrated in the church at the foot of the Viminal; he revelled in the exercise of what had been an infrequent necessity during his boyhood, but which was now an inestimable privilege.

After the conclusion of the Mass, he remained some

period of time to recall again the two days of ease when he had neglected to incite the three Irish to faith in Jesus Christ, to accuse himself, and to remember the punishment God had imposed on him. He would not permit himself to forget either his fault or the punishment; he would not permit the good fortune and pleasurableness of these months to distract his attention from alertness to the will of God.

In the spring came news that the Goths at long last had begun to attack. Romans pretended relief: "Now the legions can decimate those barbarians," was the general comment. Immediately came more news of the Goths attacking in overwhelming numbers, of repulses by the legions, of renewed attacks when the barbarians hurled their forces repeatedly against the legions' positions despite staggering losses inflicted upon them. Then came the dreaded news: The Goths had dislodged the legions and were driving them back upon Rome!

Dinners and musical entertainments ceased at the house of Senator Pinianus on the Viminal. Many men visited the house, some alone, others in groups, to discuss what they termed "the seriousness of the situation," while maintaining their confidence that these barbaric Goths could not actually intend to hurl themselves against the Invincible City. They claimed so many hours of the day that Patrick saw his patron only briefly and then in company with others.

The number who attended Mass in the church at the foot of the hill increased slightly, the faces of the newcomers clearly revealing the fear that impelled them to seek help of their God. Patrick saw the same fear in the faces of the common people in the streets. Perhaps some of them also placed their faith in God or, perhaps, like so many of those who visited the Senator, placed their faith in the thick stone walls that stood between themselves and the approaching barbarians.

Individual legionnaires—those wounded in the first battles—soon appeared in Rome. Patrick found two bearing the emblem of the Twentieth, but neither were Britons, and neither knew a decurion named Calpornius. With the assistance of the Senator, he gained admission to the buildings designated as hospitals and found more members of the Twentieth, including some from Britain; but these also asserted ignorance of any decurion named Calpornius. "I am beginning to wonder," he admitted to his patron, "if my father's unit has been annihilated."

The Senator grasped his arm encouragingly. "The legions are about two days march above the city. As soon as the Twentieth enters and establishes headquarters, we will visit the officers. They will know where to find your father." Early in the afternoon of the third day, he guided Patrick into the crowded, bustling midsection of the city to a building that displayed, above the entrance, the great shield of the Twentieth Legion.

Many officers and men were in the room they entered, the officers talking together in groups, the men waiting until ordered to some task that dispatched them to another part of the building or out through the door to the street. Senator Pinianus started to move through the press with Patrick following when a Centurion recognized him and commanded thunderously, "Make room for the Senator!" The room became silent immediately; officers and men drew away deferentially. "May I help you, Sir?" the Centurion offered.

The Senator nodded his gratitude. "We wish to locate a certain decurion, Calpornius."

The Centurion, a hard-faced veteran, shook his head quickly in token of ignorance, then bellowed the message to those thronging the room.

"I had a Decurion Calpornius in my command in Britain," a voice answered.

Patrick responded joyfully to the announcement. "He's the man," he called quickly. "Where can we find him?"

Another centurion, older than the first and shorter, emerged from the crowd. He bowed slightly to the Senator then looked at Patrick's powerful frame admiringly. "Calpornius commanded a hiberna in my district," he explained.

"Bannaventa Hiberna," Patrick added eagerly. "He's my father. Where is he now?"

The Centurion looked wonderingly at Patrick. "He had a son," he affirmed slowly, "but that son was taken by Irish raiders just before the Twentieth . . ."

"I know that part of the story very well," Patrick interrupted impatiently. "I was the son. I escaped from Ireland and came here to find my father."

The officer delayed answering, letting his expression forewarn that his reply would be disappointing. "He expected that you would escape. When the Legion withdrew from Britain, he asked to be retired so that he would be there when you escaped and returned."

"He's in Britain?" Patrick exclaimed.

The Centurion nodded. "He was when we left."

Patrick stared speechlessly at the officer, shocked by the grotesque realization that he had pursued a mere phantasm across sea and land while his father had waited confidently at Bannaventa. He felt his patron grasping his arm sympathetically and looked at him, bewildered by the absurdity.

Senator Pinianus questioned the Centurion, requiring

him to confirm his knowledge with additional details. Patrick listened without interest to the questions and answers. The Centurion's statements, especially the comment that his father had expected him to escape the Irish, were sufficient to themselves.

The habit ingrained by months of contemplation in the church at the foot of the Viminal asserted itself, and his attention veered sharply from the room and the men. Almighty God would not have sent him halfway across the world without purpose; the God who is not mocked does not mock His creatures. Why had God directed him from Ireland to Rome?

* * * * *

Automatically, Patrick preceded Senator Pinianus, forcing a path for the older man through the crowds of Romans and refugees in the street outside the headquarters building. His mind held so tenaciously to the question of God's purpose that he was hardly aware of his actions of the moment. The crowds thinned gradually until they were able to walk together.

"You must be very disappointed, Patrick," the Senator sympathized.

Patrick turned his head absently toward the older man. "I hadn't thought of disappointment," he admitted slowly. "I'm puzzled, rather than disappointed, as to why I am here." He turned his head forward and looked along the narrow roadway to the point where it turned gently to the left and began to climb the slope of the Viminal. "That may not be proper," he offered thoughtfully, wondering if his lack of disappointment might be another manifestation of his rusticity. "If I did come to Rome with the hope of finding my father, I should be disappointed."

"Patrick! Patrick!" the older man scolded. "Stop accusing yourself."

Patrick lowered his head slightly and moved it regretfully. "A man must be honest with himself." He raised his head and looked forward sightlessly while his memory sought the past. "When I made the first attempts to escape, just after I was taken to Ireland, all I thought of was returning to my father. Then, gradually, I thought less often of returning to him and more often merely of escape itself. I didn't know that I was changing my purpose. I didn't realize that it was changing until . . ." He stopped talking, unwilling to refer needlessly to the death of Victoricus. "I realized that I had changed my purpose only when I was alone, walking across Ireland."

"That was entirely natural, Patrick," the older man said emphatically. "You were only sixteen when you were taken. Your father symbolized freedom. Then you lived through years of slavery, of hardship, of brutality and danger without the assistance of your father, and you became accustomed to separation from him. You no longer needed a symbol of freedom; your mind fastened on freedom itself."

"But I was disappointed," Patrick objected, "when I learned that the Twentieth was not here in Rome—on that very first night when I entered the city and the Centurion brought me to you." He was impatient with himself that he could not say what he wished to say. He realized that he was not so rustic that he was unmindful of this other man's sensibilities. Yet, if he were both honest and capable of expressing himself properly, he could, without offense, tell the Senator that the kindnesses he had received, together with the agreeableness of life in Rome, had undermined his purpose. He was not disappointed, he admitted, because reunion with his father was no longer a necessity for his individual happiness. Here in Rome, he had freedom, he had a comfortable—indeed a luxurious—life, he enjoyed the patronage of one of Rome's leaders. In time, he would acquire social grace, and eventually feel himself equal to all the others whom now he could only admire. The prospect of such a future had beguiled and weakened him until he was not disappointed to learn that his father was not in Rome; he was, he felt guiltily, inclined in the contrary direction.

"You were disappointed," the Senator analyzed, "because you had come so far, endured so much, then found that you had done all to no purpose."

Patrick weighed briefly the explanation, then a sorry smile touched the corners of his mouth. "Not my purpose," he agreed. "But there must be some purpose, sir. Father Alexius and Victoricus convinced me that some purpose underlies every event—and they convinced me when I resisted them as stubbornly as I could."

Senator Pinianus made a throaty and unintelligible sound of agreement. They had come to the foot of the hill and he raised his hand to Patrick's shoulder, partly for assistance on the upward course of the road, partly in gesture of friendship, partly with the proprietary manner of a patron. "I can tell you one reason, Patrick. That was to reestablish an old man's faith in God at the very moment when that faith seemed completely shattered."

Patrick glanced at him sharply.

"Are you surprised, Patrick?" Senator Pinianus smiled. "You thought of Victoricus' father as a man so firmly established in faith that nothing could disturb him?" He shook his head sadly. "We speak too glibly when we speak of faith as a gift—something given to us by God without effort on our part. It is a gift—a great gift—but none of us receives it in its fullness until God tries us and tempers us and tests our faith. Our friend, Bishop Augustine, inferred something of the sort—'He Who made you without your help will not save you without your will,'" he quoted. He looked directly at Patrick. "You've seen how the smiths temper metal—from the fire into the water, back into the fire and again into the water. So also does God temper our faith.

"Oh, I once thought myself a man of very great faith—even despite the knowledge of St. Peter's presumption. When Victoricus disappeared, I began to pray—earnestly, devoutly, persistently and, above all, confidently. I prayed very much during the first months after he disappeared. But, as the months increased, my hopes declined; as my hopes declined, my prayers changed until I made them into demands upon God. A day finally came when I discovered that I had become bitter—very bitter.

"I was bitter towards God Who had taken my wife from me, then my one child, and had, moreover, taken my child in such an extraordinary manner that I didn't know whether he lived or died. I hoped that he was dead, but I tormented myself with thoughts that he was alive and enslaved by the Irish barbarians.

"I couldn't endure those torments but I couldn't pray without suffering them because my prayers revived them. So I abandoned prayer except during short intervals when I felt sufficiently strong to endure the torments of uncertainty. Those intervals occurred less and less frequently—I foresaw a time approaching when I should become as mute as God was deaf.

"But, deep in my soul, I dreaded the day when I should lose faith completely in God. I made one last desperate effort. I prayed that God would either return Victoricus or assure me, by any device He chose, that Victoricus was dead."

Patrick waited expectantly for the older man to continue. He glanced at him after a moment but the Senator seemed content that his explanation sufficed. "So I came to Rome," said Patrick thoughtfully, "because I was the only one who could tell you certainly about Victoricus." His voice lowered wonderingly. "God sent Victoricus to Ireland with me so that I might gain the faith I had ignored during my childhood. Then God sent me here to Rome to assist your faith. Yet He did both under concealment of other incidents and other motives."

The discovery of God's hidden operations stirred Patrick. He had recognized, gratefully, the gift of faith received from God under the stress of slavery in Ireland; he had not sought other reasons for his captivity and subsequent release—he had not suspected that God had other reasons until the night when he had been delivered from the Suevi and escorted into Rome only to learn that his father was not there. He was startled by the discovery that he had served God's purpose when he had thought he merely pursued his own.

What of the future—what was expected of him? Could he remain in Rome and continue to enjoy this life? Must not his father long ago have become convinced that he was dead?

But Senator Pinianus had never become convinced that Victoricus was dead until the only human who could convince had come. Patrick remembered the expression of relief he had seen when he told the Senator, in the middle of that first night, that Victoricus had died. "Certainty is better than uncertainty," the Senator had said. His father might have said the same had Victoricus been the one to escape and visit Bannaventa.

And that Centurion at the headquarters—"He expected that you would escape," he had said. So confident had his father been that he had resigned from the Legion in order that he might be at Bannaventa when his son returned.

Reluctantly, Patrick viewed the course required of him. He was not free, as he had thought, to pursue his own ends. He was free to pursue his own ends only when they did not conflict with God's law. God's law now demanded of him that he honor his father, not alone with his lips, but with his physical presence in Britain. Only by obeying God's law could he be sure that he served God's purposes. The search for his father had already served one of God's purposes by bringing him to Rome and to Senator Pinianus; he must resume that search. He turned slightly to the other, climbing the Hill beside him, and opened his lips to speak of renewing his search. He almost spoke before he became aware of the hand clinging to his shoulder.

There was nothing unusual about the hand nor its grasp; his patron had done the same as often as they had climbed the slope of the Viminal together. It was the very ordinary action of an aged man. Yet, there seemed something different this once—whether actually in his patron's manner of grasping his shoulder, as though the hand conveyed a message of its own, or in his mind. He closed his lips without speaking.

He had never had reason to consider that the Senator regarded him differently than he had regarded the Senator—he had been so preoccupied with his own goal and had held anticipated reunion with his father so prominently before him that he had not noticed, or had not properly evaluated, repeated evidences of the Senator's interest in him. Now the simple gesture of a hand holding to his shoulder awakened him.

How stupid! how unobserving he had been! The Senator had given him the room once occupied by Victoricus, had shielded him willingly during the social gatherings, had sought his views and comments concerning the guests, had helped to lessen his rusticity by drawing him into conversations about Bishop Augustine, the city, the army of great Rome and innumerable other subjects. In all these things, the Senator had gone far beyond mere courtesy to a youth who had been a companion of his one son.

What course was now required of him? Was he to "honor his father" despite the pain he would inflict on his patron, or remain gratefully with this aging man and be the son he desired?

They gained the top of the Hill and entered the formal garden through the heavy stone arch covered over with ivy. Pinianus let his hand drop wearily from the shoulder that had assisted him. They followed the straight paths, bordered with carefully trimmed boxwood, and gained the shaded loggia.

Senator Pinianus sat down on a stone bench, his back to the wall of the house, and motioned for Patrick to sit beside him. "I suppose . . ."

A faint cry, as from a great distance, interrupted him. A louder cry, marked with anger, followed immediately. Senator Pinianus and Patrick looked northward from their vantage point, across a wooded area, toward the city wall— toward the very gate through which Patrick had entered Rome.

"The Goths," Pinianus murmured. "The men on the walls have sighted them."

New cries sounded from other points along the wall.

The Senator arose and stood uncertainly. "We expected only their advance units," he exclaimed, "but their main body must have arrived. The city is surrounded!"

Patrick felt a reaction completely at variance with the Senator's alarm—a reaction of relief. He was spared the necessity of choosing between duty to his father and gratitude to this aged man who had befriended and favored him. God had willed that he be confined within Rome's walls! He stood up, took his patron's arm lightly and urged him toward the entrance to the house. "You should rest, sir. You will have considerable work in coming days."

Senator Pinianus yielded to the direction. He looked again toward the city wall as he moved. "There is no work for the Senate now," he observed quietly. "The military must do all."

9

CONTRARY to the expectations of the Senator, there was no military activity. Rome's legionnaires and auxiliaries manned the walls and watched alertly for signs of assault by the Goths who ringed the city but remained just beyond bowshot. The first week of June brought a wave of heat across the sea from Africa, but the barbarians surrounding Rome held to their positions and showed no indication of returning to the cooler north nor of attacking the walls. They seemed willing to besiege the city indefinitely.

The dread of uncertainty settled upon Rome. Citizens and refugees continued to crowd the streets in the center of the city, shuffling restlessly and purposelessly but without inclination to talk. Any sound that might be interpreted as an alarm was sufficient to stop all movement; the crowd waited fearfully until time assured that the Goths had not yet attacked. Slowly, at first, then more rapidly, their dejection gave way to the desperation of despair; they muttered hopefully that the attack would begin and bring an end to their torment.

In the beginning of June's second week, a new spirit seized the crowds: If the Goths would not attack, the legions must! To quiet them, a detachment of legionnaires attempted a night assault against enemy positions along the southern wall; but Goth sentries were alert, and Goth warriors overwhelmed and decimated the detachment. The failure of that night convinced Roman crowds of what they had refused to contemplate—that the Goths did not intend to vitiate their strength by futile assault but were determined to starve the city until it surrendered. A spirit of panic grew among those imprisoned within the city, and they raised a new cry: Let the Senate convene—let it treat with the besieging Goths and pay whatever ransom is necessary to end the siege and assure delivery of Rome.

Patrick accompanied Senator Pinianus to the Senate chamber and, as companion—though he was termed a secretary—was permitted to sit beside his patron on the long, curving bench instead of being shunted to the crowded gallery. He knew, as did all Rome, the public demands which had caused this extraordinary session; but he looked on it as a device by which the Senate sought to soothe the frightened populace. He looked about covertly at the faces of the assembled legislators, perhaps sixty in all, conscious that he was looking on the assembly that ruled the world.

One senator mounted the rostrum. In measured tones and artificial deliberateness, he reviewed Rome's "unhappy situation" and distress of "her people." After considerable time, he proposed appointment of a committee to treat with "those beyond the walls."

Other senators followed the first. Patrick's impatience grew as, one after another, they spoke approvingly of the action proposed by their "honored colleague" and urged "this august body" to preserve "Immortal Rome."

Patrick moved restlessly on the bench as each speaker disappointed him. His expression must have revealed his mounting disgust, for Senator Pinianus grasped his hand, warning him to calmness. The youth forced himself to sit stiffly erect and motionless while he endured the farce of men who sought by pretense to preserve the appearance rather than the reality of Rome's greatness. This was not that great Rome on which the Christian world depended— the Rome his father had served and which, in his boyhood, he had dreamed of serving; for that Rome which he had conceived in his mind would have died gloriously and magnificently; never would it have surrendered ignominiously by purchasing its freedom from a barbaric host.

A lull intruded into the proceedings; the presiding officer inquired gravely whether other gentlemen wished to be heard. Patrick looked expectantly at his patron, but Senator Pinianus did not move. The presiding officer asked calmly a "showing of hands by those members who approved the proposed action;" hands were raised, but Senator Pinianus let his rest, folded together in his lap. The session ended.

Two other Senators joined them, returned with them to the Viminal, and remained for dinner. When the guests departed, Senator Pinianus put his arm through Patrick's and guided him to the loggia. "I need not ask your reaction, but I may be able to restore myself in your esteem."

Patrick felt embarrassed that his patron had construed his restlessness and evident disgust as directed to himself. Once again, he was conscious of his rusticity—his inability to conceal his inner emotions—his inability now to express himself properly. "I knew you did not favor the formation of that committee," he exclaimed. "Neither did those other two gentlemen."

"But you did wonder why we did not express our objections."

They sat together on the bench that faced out over the city, now invisible under the cloak of the soft summer night; the moon had not yet appeared, and the city lay hidden in darkness the stars could not relieve. To the right, small points of light marked the progress of officers inspecting the men at their positions along the wall; beyond the wall, great flames leaped high as though the Goths already celebrated their triumph.

"I did not favor formation of that committee," Senator Pinianus agreed. "Neither did these others who were with us this evening. But, Patrick, three men cannot range themselves effectively against the overwhelming majority. Had we spoken, a few more might have joined themselves to us—had all the senators felt completely free, perhaps you would have seen a majority opposed to this plan. The greater number of those present today considered that they must either submit to the wishes of the people and treat with the enemy or be confronted with anarchy, mob violence—even treachery."

"Treachery!" Patrick exclaimed.

"There are always some who treasure their lives and property above honor."

Patrick gazed on the great fires that lighted the hills above the city. Perhaps the fires, perhaps the proceedings of the day, perhaps his knowledge of the craven fear that had seized upon Rome, perhaps all of these reminded him of another night, another fire and other people who, like these Romans, had let their love for life and the ease of paying ransom undermine their spirit.

In slow, resentful tones, Patrick told of the girl who had died rather than suffer dishonor while men around her had suffered dishonor rather than die. "I thought that what I saw that night—the cowardice of the men because of their willingness to await a time when they would be ransomed—was something I would never witness again. Now . . ." He released his breath noisily in token of contempt. He stopped talking, aware that his indignation might incite statements offensive to his patron. He would not permit his rusticity to affront the Senator a second time.

The other waited some moments, letting the silence of the night calm Patrick's indignation. He knew well the idealism of youth, good in itself, evil in its compulsion to reckless speech or action. He knew the futility of opposing that overwhelming force as he knew the futility of opposing overwhelming numbers. "History repeats, over and over," he said after a time, "that civilization contains within itself the seed of demoralization. Civilization is the securing of individual rights by enforcement of law. It brings in its train greater productiveness and, therefore, greater comfort. It brings leisure—time not required for labor; time that may be given to religion, study, relaxation and other good activities; but time which the majority waste away in idleness and the excessive pursuit of pleasure. As that continues, people become more firmly attached to the pleasures of life and increasingly more reluctant to sacrifice those pleasures for the sake of honor, love, and the nobler qualities. They become more and more demoralized. When demoralization is sufficiently advanced, those civilized people are subjugated by the uncivilized." He paused momentarily, then added dolefully, "We may be witnessing that now."

Patrick looked into the darkness toward the sound of his patron's voice. He wanted to protest the repugnant analysis, but the desire brought vividly to mind the night when Victoricus had told him of assaults by the barbarians against the Empire. He had not wanted to believe—he had even told Victoricus he would not believe. He realized that he was about to repeat the same words to this man, the father of Victoricus, even though he did believe. "But the Church," he muttered, seeking an escape. "If Rome falls, what of the Church?"

Roman pride tinged the Senator's retort. "If Rome's legionnaires could not destroy the Church by crucifying Jesus, Patrick, these barbarians cannot do it by destroying Christians or their churches." His robes rustled softly as he arose from the bench. "I'm weary, Patrick," he murmured. His sandals scraped on the stones of the loggia; the sounds diminished as he went through the doorway into the house.

Patrick remained on his bench, staring sightlessly into the night, blind alike to the great fires of the Goths and the points of light moving along the city wall. The lessons of history might explain the conduct of these people in the city before him; they could not alleviate the pain of disillusionment. He could have accepted the military defeat of Rome as the misfortune of war; he revolted against a people who willingly subjected themselves to an enemy and pleaded that they be permitted to ransom themselves.

*   *   *   *   *

During the days that followed, emissaries of the Senate trudged out daily from the city. Crowds congregated within the gates, awaiting their return, questioning them when they appeared. Day succeeded day; the emissaries became worn and tired, the crowds more sullen.

Senator Pinianus remained in his own apartment

through much of those days—"resting," he termed it.
"I seem always to be weary," he repeated in a puzzled
voice. He seemed pleased when Patrick, on the second day,
brought Bishop Augustine's book and settled himself on
a bench in the room so that he could read while his patron
slept, or talk when the other awakened. Patrick attributed
the Senator's indisposition to the heat of the season, but as
his patron displayed no improvement, suggested that they
call the physician. The Senator refused. "I need only rest,"
he said confidently.

On the eighth day, the committee members returned
from the camp of the Goths much earlier than had been
their custom; their expressions indicated some success, but
they refused to answer the questions of the crowd. "We
must report to the Senate," they insisted, which was sufficient to inform the crowd that they had been successful.
The impatience of the mob, together with the heat of the
daylight hours, spurred the Senate to convene that very evening to hear the report.

Patrick attempted, somewhat timidly, to dissuade Senator Pinianus from attending the session. He was reluctant to
state his true reason and invented an excuse: "It will be like
attending the funeral of Rome."

Senator Pinianus dismissed the suggestion. As long as
he continued to be a member of the Senate, he would dis-
charge his responsibility by attending the sessions.

Again they sat together on the long, curved bench. The
chamber was very warm with the heat of the day and those
that had preceded it. The crowds in the gallery added their
own heat. Even the lighting wicks, floating on their little
lakes of oil, seemed to contribute their own mite to the
discomfort.

That senator who had first proposed negotiating with "those beyond the walls" and had, therefore, been appointed leader of the committee, walked solemnly to the rostrum. "I am happy to inform this august body," he began encouragingly, "that your committee has achieved a certain success." He continued for some minutes with his verbose recitation until the chamber became expectantly quiet; then he began the reading of the enemy's demands for gold, silver, jewels, silks, pepper—"one third to be paid immediately, another third on the same date in 409, the final third one year later."

A shocked silence possessed the room until several senators cried out their protests in unison, only to be countered immediately by other and opposed shouts from those massed in the gallery.

Patrick held himself tensely still, his face expressionless. These senators had once bowed to the will of this mob when they had appointed and empowered this committee, which now returned with terms they denounced as ruinous to them and to every wealthy man in Rome. He felt an interior satisfaction that, having acceded once to the mob at the cost of Rome's greatness, they must bow again at the cost of their own fortunes. Remorse followed swiftly— the misfortune visited on some senators was visited on all, including his own patron. He glanced stealthily at the Senator to discover his reaction to the proceedings.

The Senator sat very erect as always, but his tightly pressed lips drew long lines down the length of his face. He was exhausting his strength merely by sitting.

Patrick returned his gaze to the speaker on the rostrum at the front of the chamber, wondering uncertainly whether he might disrupt the proceedings by insisting that his patron

leave. Some Senator shouted angrily, "What will those barbarians leave us?"

Patrick was surprised to hear Senator Pinianus bark the
answer, "They will leave you your lives." The mob in the
gallery hooted derisively. Senator Pinianus touched Patrick's arm and motioned that they should leave.

The night air, sufficiently warm itself, seemed cold
after the intense warmth of the chamber. Patrick drew a
deep breath, enjoying the sensation of coolness as the air
struck his robes, wet with perspiration. He was distracted
immediately by concern for his patron, whose older body
would suffer rather than enjoy the sudden change. "I should
have brought a robe for you," he apologized.

Senator Pinianus grumbled once, then let his grumble
change to a bitter laugh. "My temper is enough cloak tonight,
Patrick. I endured as much as I could of their hypocrisy."

The vehemence of the older man surprised Patrick. He
had never before heard the other give way to anger. He
found hope that the night air was benefiting his patron.

"I could not endure their cries any longer," the Senator
continued. "They cry of being ruined when they know their
fortunes will suffer nothing more than a severe injury. Not
one of them will be ruined. But all of them have become
money merchants, whatever else each may call himself.
They measure their stature by the amount of their wealth;
they forget they are Roman."

Patrick felt dumbfounded by the disclosure. "And they
need pay only one third now," he said wonderingly. He felt
a sudden return of the disgust he had experienced on the
night after the Senate had formed and authorized its committee: disgust for both the mobs of Rome and those senators distinguished from the mob only by their wealth.

A slight sound, unmistakably that of a man seized by illness, made him turn swiftly and reach fumblingly in the darkness for his patron. The older man had collapsed. Patrick lifted the limp form and hurried, half-running, to the Viminal.

*   *   *   *   *

Senator Pinianus was very ill, the physician indicated when he completed his examination. He moved from the couch and led Patrick from the apartment. For a moment, he seemed to study Patrick, obviously appraising the youth's rights, then deciding against them. "I will inform the Senator's nephews," he said stiffly.

"I have already sent servants to them, Sir. And I sent other servants to notify the presiding officer of the Senate and those gentlemen whom the Senator seemed to regard as his more intimate friends."

He resented the physician's manner. The man clearly indicated that he regarded Patrick as an interloper. He enjoyed the slight surprise he caused the man; but he was more anxious to obtain the physician's promise to return in the early morning than to enjoy his own small pleasure.

When the other departed, Patrick returned to the apartment of his patron. A servant sat very quietly within the door. Patrick stood near the couch, looking down anxiously on the pallid face and watching the rapid rise and fall of the Senator's chest. One of the small oil lamps flickered, and he motioned to the servant to bring another. The man hesitated as though challenging Patrick's right to issue an order. Patrick half-turned in a threatening manner—he had not forgotten the value of pretended anger when treating with servants—and the man hurried to his task. Patrick turned again to his patron.

He heard the door open again and thought that the servant had reentered the room until a touch on his arm caused him to turn and discover the Senator's two nephews, who apparently had arrived together. They nodded curtly, looked down briefly on the form of their uncle, then motioned Patrick to accompany them from the room.

Patrick felt no misgivings when he went with the two and related in detail all the physician had told him. These two were his patron's nephews and most closely related to him; justice required that they be informed fully.

"Has my uncle completed his will?"

Patrick felt a sudden surge of animosity, even contempt. For the first time, he realized fully why these two—he had always ignored their manner towards him because of their diminutive stature—had endeavored to humiliate him whenever opportunity offered. "I know nothing of that," he answered sharply.

"He had a considerable number of valuables," the other nephew interjected. "Items of gold and precious stones, and some gold coins. Are they in a safe place?" This man's tone was offensively demanding and suspicious.

Patrick smiled derisively. "They must be. I've never seen them."

The nephew looked at him piercingly, obviously unhappy that he had disclosed the existence of the items. He seemed about to propound other questions, but his brother forestalled him by grasping his arm and drawing him toward the doorway leading from the house. "Patrick knows nothing of Uncle's affairs," he said pointedly.

Patrick did not accompany them to the door. He stood, looking after them contemptuously. By their manner alone, they had made themselves one with those of the Senate whom Senator Pinianus had denounced this very night as men who "measure their stature by the amount of their wealth; they forget that they are Roman." He returned to the apartment of the Senator, told the servant that he might call another to relieve him—an order the man obeyed readily—lifted a bench near to his patron's couch and settled himself to watch through the night. The Senator opened his eyes, looked briefly at Patrick without speaking, then closed them again contentedly.

*   *   *   *   *

During seven days, the Senator awakened infrequently and remained awake only as long as necessary to drink the liquid food ordered by the physician and a small amount of wine. At the end of the week, he spoke for the first time, but so indistinctly—as the physician had foretold—that Patrick understood his meaning only from the movements of his eyes and weak motions of his hands. From that time, however, his strength increased.

Patrick welcomed each indication of improvement. By scowling threateningly and giving blunt orders, he had imposed his will on the servants of the household so that all of them were afraid to slacken their efforts. He knew they resented him; he knew that the physician continued to regard him as an interloper; he knew that the two nephews looked upon him antagonistically. He wished his patron would recover speedily and once again assume direction of his own household.

He would not remain longer than necessary, Patrick had determined. The Goths had withdrawn to the north of Italy, where they intended to await complete payment of Rome's ransom; the country to the south was open and free of raiders—he could go southward and find passage on a ship to Britain.

Weeks became months. Winter was firmly settled over Rome before Senator Pinianus was able to leave his couch for short intervals, though he was able to lie awake and talk clearly for long periods with his nephews and the friends who visited him—periods when Patrick was able to withdraw to his own apartment and sleep so that he could maintain his nightly vigils. When the warm days of spring swept over Rome, Senator Pinianus had recovered sufficiently that he was able to spend the daylight hours on a couch prepared for him on the loggia. It was there he first spoke to Patrick of the certainty of approaching death.

"You are recovering steadily," Patrick said emphatically.

The Senator agreed. "For the time," he answered without interest. "But I am not such a fool, Patrick, as to forget my age." He raised his hand to stop Patrick's objections. "And I've not been so sick that I have not seen the manner of—let us say, certain people—towards you. The physician, certain of my friends . . ."

"Some have been very good to me," Patrick countered. He wished to calm him.

"A few." Senator Pinianus regarded him steadily. "Most of them haven't tried to ease your tasks here or make your stay in Rome as pleasant as it might have been. Are you anxious to leave?"

The direct question discomfited Patrick. He was anxious to leave, but he would not abandon his invalid patron.

His goal—the goal that had remained before him since the first days of his captivity in Ireland—still lay before him. He had not been anxious to leave Rome for that one reason; he had become anxious to leave only because of his increasing contempt and disgust for the Romans—commoners and nobles alike. "I had thought—after you recover," he said awkwardly.

Senator Pinianus motioned with his hands toward his prostrate form on the couch. "This is as much as I can hope to recover. Oh, I shall probably walk a little again," he added, "but I shall spend more of my time here than anywhere else. You believe that you must go to Britain?" His voice had become plaintive.

Patrick smiled reassuringly. "Someday, sir. But not until you have recovered sufficiently and not until one of your nephews can arrange to live here with you and care for you."

Senator Pinianus grunted unpleasantly. "My nephews are arranging their affairs to leave Rome and sail to Africa," he said scathingly.

The announcement surprised Patrick. He had heard that some wealthy Romans were leaving the city, removing whatever they could of their wealth rather than sacrifice a great part of it to the Goths. He had not known that the Senator's own nephews planned to flee.

"Patrick!" the Senator interrupted his reverie. "Go to my apartment," he ordered. "Lock the door and draw the drapes over the windows so that none can see. Pull my couch from its position and you will find that one end rests on a stone flag that is loosened from the others. Take the bag that you will find beneath that stone, replace the stone and put everything in order."

Patrick had little light when he had complied with the instructions of his patron, but his sense of touch was sufficient to identify the contents of the leather bag beneath the stone as the valuables mentioned months before by the Senator's nephew. Carefully he restored the apartment and carried the bag, concealed by his flowing sleeves from the chance sight of others, to the Senator.

Senator Pinianus moved his head, refusing the bag. "That's yours, Patrick," he said shortly. "With that, you can buy passage or buy your own boat to take you to Britain."

The bag in Patrick's hands seemed suddenly to increase in weight. As quickly, the soft, flexible leather became an obnoxious and detestable thing. He stood dumbly, holding the bag of treasure carelessly in his hand still outstretched toward his patron while the pain of injustice struck within. He frowned. He had not served his patron for this; he had given no cause for his patron to think that he had served him for this.

Then memory stirred and transformed the leather bag in his hand into another leather bundle that Victoricus had thrust into his hands—the bag containing the weapons. A new joy raced through him, driving away the pain and all else but the realization that this father and his dead son were more identical than he—or they—had known. A broad smile of delight supplanted his frown. He sat down on a bench facing his patron and dropped the bag of treasure between his feet. "I will go to Britain, sir. But I will wait until you depart for Africa with your nephews."

Senator Pinianus looked at him gravely, surprised by the spirit of impudence he had never suspected in Patrick. Then he understood, and his graveness gave way to an answering smile.

Patrick touched the leather bag disdainfully with his foot. "I will replace this so that we can share it at the proper time—when you depart for Africa and I for Britain."

10

THROUGH the spring and summer of 409, the departure of Rome's wealthier families, including several members of the Senate, continued in a steady trickle. Commoners began to grumble—the more gifted among them fulminated publicly; but the greater number were mollified by a resolution of the Senate censuring those who fled as "timorous, cowardly and unworthy Romans."

In July, a cavalcade of burdened carts and drivers, guarded by legionnaires and their officers, carried northward the second portion of the ransom demanded by the Goths and returned without incident. When the rainy season arrived in October, bringing an end even to the trickle of those fleeing to Africa, all Rome felt a renewal of hopefulness: With payment of the final portion of the ransom in 410, they could expect deliverance.

Perhaps the dream of deliverance, perhaps mere latent resentment against those who fled, perhaps the flight of a few more of the wealthy in December when the rains stopped—for whatever reason, the masses of Rome awakened to the knowledge of their power and the corresponding subservience of the Senate. They demanded, and the Senate dutifully enacted, a statute depriving of their citizenship and privileges all who had fled the city. Several more wealthy families fled, and the masses demanded a statute prohibiting anyone from leaving the city without express permission of the Senate—a statute which, in actual effect, only resulted in the payment of bribes to the soldiers at the gates without interrupting the continuing trickle of escapees. The masses reacted indignantly but vainly.

All Rome recognized the growing spirit of rebellion. Servants in the great houses obeyed their masters' orders sullenly and performed their duties slowly. Tradesmen reported a rapid increase of thefts from their establishments. None ventured into the streets at night unless impelled by most serious emergencies, and then with private guards protecting them.

Two commoners claimed they had discovered soldiers in the very act of closing the little-used Metrovian Gate after permitting still another family to escape. A riot developed between the legionnaires and citizens, ending in brutal beating of commoners by the soldiers and ill will between the two classes.

Wealthy families who had resigned themselves to the sacrifice required of them by the Goths watched fearfully the signs of increasing civil unrest; in March, the trickle of escapees broke suddenly into a flood of such proportions that the Senate itself was reduced by more than half. Before the exodus ended in mid-April, Rome realized that so much wealth had been removed by those who fled, the city would be unable to deliver the final portion of the ransom demanded by the Goths.

Pope and priests pleaded that Romans turn their minds and hearts to God—put their trust in Him. Few heard because so few attended the churches; fewer heeded.

Panic swept over the city and a new madness seized the people: Let the civil authorities appease the pagan gods of ancient Rome! Let them arrange a ceremony of propitiation on Capitol Hill! The demand swelled until a timid Senate dared no longer to refuse and solemnly authorized a committee to consult Pope Innocent and ask his views.

"No!" the Pope thundered. "Rome may no longer be the City of Greatness, but it must always be the City of God."

At the house on the Viminal, Senator Pinianus and Patrick received the news of those who fled, of the temper of the people, of rumors and facts, from those of the Senator's friends who called regularly to visit and consult him. The household itself suffered none of the difficulties experienced by other great families—Patrick's scowl and voice effectively cowed those who might have displayed sullenness, and incited activity in those who might have neglected their duties; the Senator listened, with increasing annoyance, to stories of the conditions tolerated in other houses—conditions offered as an excuse for fleeing Rome. For that reason, he welcomed the report of Pope Innocent's blunt answer. "There is at least one man in Rome who does not fear the mob."

"He does not fear the Goths either," the informant added. "He rode out of the city before dawn this morning, leaving an announcement that he has gone northward to seek an extension of time from the Goths. During his absence, he asks all Rome to pray continuously."

"I wish he had told them to pray while they can but fight if they must," the Senator muttered darkly.

The remark surprised the visitor. "They will if the Goths attack," he answered confidently.

Senator Pinianus shook his head doubtfully. "I doubt that they will attack," he said grimly. "If they had intended to attack, they would have attacked two years ago instead of sitting outside the walls. They don't want this city; they want the wealth that is in it. If they refuse an extension of time and move against Rome, it will reveal clearly that they have already arranged a method of entering. Fools might attack the walls; these Goths are barbarians, but they are not fools."

"Do you mean that some within Rome . . . ?"

"Exactly. I mean that there are some within the city who will accept a bribe to admit the Goths as readily as others gave bribes in order to escape from the city."

The blunt words clearly displeased the visitor. His manner indicated that had such a statement been made by a person of lesser stature and importance, he would have denounced him. He contented himself by inventing a reason for immediate departure.

Patrick accompanied the man to the door. When he returned to the room, the Senator was sitting dejectedly, leaning back listlessly in his wicker chair; his attitude suggested that he did not wish to be disturbed, and Patrick continued to the loggia.

He could understand his patron's reaction—the born Roman was already grieving for Rome. He sat on a bench and looked down on the city beneath the hill—a city that lay bright and beautiful in the warm sunlight—a city deceptively great, deceptively noble, deceptively confident. He could not share his patron's dejection: The Senator had known the reality of Rome's stature, while he had known it only as a dream. The dream had dissipated during the two years since he had arrived; he had become completely disillusioned.

The thought of his own goal returned to him. He had thought of it only infrequently since the time when he had determined that duty required him to remain with his patron; when he had thought of it, he had contemplated it as something of a pleasant diversion—let it entertain him. He did not regret that he had remained to care for the Senator, but he knew that, except for this one influence, he would have departed gladly.

Consideration of the future did not occur to him. Later he would say of himself, "I know not how to provide for the future." He lacked that imagination which induces foolhardy dreams or vitiating fears, or which disturbs its possessor by distracting him from matters of present importance. He could consider only that which was intimately related to the present.

They had few days to await news from the north. A charioteer rode into the city, two weeks after departure of the Pope to cry the alarm, "The Goths are moving southward. They thrust the Pope into Ravenna—they stationed guards to keep him there."

Senator Pinianus received the news calmly, as something he had expected. He was in his apartment, resting on his couch, when Patrick brought the information. For a long time, he said nothing. He let his gaze move from object to object in the room, from window to door to decorated ceiling, after the manner of a man recalling pleasures of the past associated with what he saw. At length, he looked at Patrick. "You have not forgotten your leather bag?" He had lowered his voice so that the servant seated outside the door would not hear.

Involuntarily, Patrick glanced downward toward the flagstones beneath the couch. He smiled slightly. "Our leather bag," he corrected.

Senator Pinianus ignored the whimsical answer. He lay back on the couch and looked upward. "I hope God does not demand that I watch Rome die."

Patrick's smile faded. He groped awkwardly for a means of diverting the older man as once before, so long ago, he had tried to find words for diverting this man's son from the contemplation of death.

"I'll sleep for a time," the Senator added before Patrick could speak.

Patrick retreated quietly to his accustomed bench in the corner of the room from which he could look out idly on the flat terrace that fronted the house or, by turning his head slightly, glance at his patron. Something that was neither sound nor movement attracted his attention, and he looked back quickly at the outstretched form. "Summon the physician!" he cried to the servant beyond the door, even as he leaped to the couch.

Neither he nor the physician were necessary, he knew immediately. God had granted the Senator's prayer.

*   *   *   *   *

Few attended the funeral of Senator Pinianus, fewer remained in the church until the body had been lowered into the crypt beneath the stone flooring and the heavy slab replaced. Patrick remained until the last mourner had departed, then walked purposefully up the slope to the house atop the Viminal.

He went first to his patron's apartment, then to his own. When he left, he had exchanged his soft, flowing robes for tough, durable hunting garments; he carried a leather coat under his arm, rolled around the weapons he would need; he had hidden the leather bag beneath his shirt; he carried a larger leather bag of food on his shoulder. He walked down the hill to the church, glanced back at the house that was no longer his home but the property of the state, and reentered the darkened church that must be his home until a way opened from Rome—northward toward France or westward to the sea.

Few others were there—it was their presence that had determined his action—and others came in following days as the Goths drew nearer to the city. A few prayed; the greater number distracted themselves from thoughts of the approaching danger by talking or games. Most had come, not because of faith in God or their own spirit of piety, but because the Goths had respected the Pope by confining him at Ravenna and would respect the churches of Rome. There were among them as many pagans as Christians.

Patrick held himself apart from the others—from those who prayed because he did not want to disturb them nor be disturbed while he prayed, from those who revelled because they revolted him. In the beginning, a sensation of hypocrisy pricked him as he remembered the days when he had been as unmindful of God as these people were; for a time he wondered if he should attempt to remind them of God and salvation, but he gave up the thought as the crowd increased.

Fear silenced even the most abandoned of those in the church on the night when the Goths entered the city. They listened tensely to the sounds of fighting as the legionnaires rushed to repair the treacherous opening—they could measure the steadily mounting volume of shouts and curses as the Goths pushed back the city's defenders—they heard the sounds change from those of battle to those of flight and pursuit. A wild chant, the victory song of the savage Goths, swelled gradually from the thousands of tribesmen plunging their way into every section of the city.

Four legionnaires darted into the church and stumbled over the unseen forms of others until they were some distance from the entrance. A band of Goths, savagely dressed in animal skins, flourishing spears and great bull-hide shields, and carrying torches, followed, but stopped abruptly as their torches lighted the area nearest to the door. One, apparently a commander, spoke an order to the others; there was some argument among them, but the leader pushed them roughly backward, and they disappeared into the night. A woman sobbed, a man laughed raucously, then the church was again silent.

For eight days, the Goths slaughtered those who resisted their quest for money, food, wine and women—then slaughtered without greater motive than sheer delight; for eight days they sated their appetites for no greater reason than sheer gluttony and lust; for the same eight days, they pretended ignorance of those huddled within the churches. As day followed day without harm or threat, those within the church at the foot of the Viminal reverted to their previous occupations—some to prayer, more to revelry.

The orgy of blood and lust exhausted itself. The main body of Goths withdrew to march southward, leaving only a garrison force to retain control of the defeated, submissive city. Romans crept forth from homes and churches to look upon their looted city and resume a life that had lost all savor. Reports arrived periodically of the Goths' unimpeded progress as they pushed southward to the ports from which they could sail to attack Africa and the last bastions of the Empire. Romans had ample reason to fear as they contemplated a future of subjection to these savage people.

Patrick remained in the church at the foot of the hill, reluctant to seek other lodgings which would force him to mingle with the bulk of the Romans. He waited patiently. He let his thoughts center on the building that sheltered him, and on all the other churches of the city which had proved havens to those who entered them. He accepted slowly the marvel that, though Rome had died, these churches had remained inviolate—symbols that the Church lived, assurance that the Church would always live of itself and needed neither protection nor support of the State. In those days, as he lost the last remnants of faith in the Roman State, he achieved the fullness of faith in the Roman Church.

A new report revived Rome: The Goths were returning northward in some disorder. A storm had destroyed the boats assembled for their conquest of Africa; their gifted leader—the genius who had welded all their tribes into one great aggressive force—was dead. Now they sought only to return to the safety of their homeland above the Alps. A band of noble Roman youths, their courage and daring enlivened by news of the enemy's adversities, fell upon and slaughtered the garrison. Other men, inspired by the example of the few, manned Rome's walls once again to bar return of the Goths. Rome was free again! Rome the magnificent, Rome the mistress of the earth, Rome the eternal, had risen from the death of oppression and slavery!

The hailing of the crowds sounded as empty noises in Patrick's ears. He could never again think of Rome as once he had—magnificent, eternal. The words belonged properly, not to Rome, but to Rome's Church, because it was God's Church.

The hordes of Goths swept rapidly past the city. Columns of legionnaires, dispatched from the city to report the movements of the barbarians, returned messengers with the news that the Goths continued northward without pause.

Early in November, the last of the enemy disappeared into the Alpine passes, and the legionnaires began the work of rebuilding the fortifications which would bar a new invasion.

Shortly before dawn, in mid-November, Patrick passed through that gate of the city which faced westward toward the port of Ostia and the sea. The sentries at the gate inspected him curiously, surprised that a man, however strong and well armed, would venture from the city alone, despite assurances that the country was completely free of hostile forces.

Patrick walked quickly but alertly, aware of danger but without fear of men. God had led him to Rome; now God had released him from Rome and would protect him. In later years he would comment of those days, "The fear of God was my guide through France and Italy and the islands of the Tyrrhenian Sea."

11

"AND, after a few years," Patrick related laconically in his *Confession*, "I was in Britain with my people, who welcomed me as their kinsman."

The countryside was as he remembered it, the village of Bannaventa and his father's villa unchanged. There were children he had never seen, but he remembered and recognized all those he had known, despite the changes wrought in their appearance during the ten years of his absence. His father had changed more than others—and for the better, Patrick knew immediately—but he had lost none of his expansiveness of manner nor his authoritative leadership.

"You will see one change, Patrick," his father said late in the evening when they had been together several days. They sat facing each other before the small fire that warded off the chill of the spring night, resting from the exertion of receiving and recognizing and embracing and talking with all who had come to greet Patrick as one who had returned from the dead. "You may already have seen it. I don't know how you may regard it, but all of us who remained here know it is a good change and want to preserve it."

Patrick studied his father curiously. His father seemed to be warning him against opposing what he described as a change—a change that must indeed be good if it were related to the subtle change in his father.

Decurion—the villagers without exception addressed him by his military title—Decurion Calpornius looked into the fire, striving for words to express his thoughts, hopeful that what he said would not arouse antagonism, yet determined that the words must be spoken. "That raid by the Irish, on the night when you were taken, was only the beginning of troubles for us. After the Twentieth withdrew, the Irish returned regularly to raid Britain. They never returned here, thanks to God, but we never knew when they might return, and we did know how defenseless we were." He turned his head slowly from the fire and faced Patrick. "We learned to be Christians in those days—something we should have done long before. We learned . . ." He stopped, obviously unable to express himself as he wished.

Patrick leaned forward slightly. "You learned how dependent we are on the mercy and providence of God?" Patrick questioned. A slow smile lighted his face at his father's surprise. "Oh, they are not my words," he denied quickly. "I learned them from a young Roman in Ireland."

Decurion Calpornius looked hopefully at his son. "You've learned what they mean and believe what they mean?"

Patrick nodded soberly. "I learned and I believe," he said simply. "We wouldn't listen to Father Alexius, so God made us fear Him in order that we would know Him and hear His priests." For the first time since he returned, Patrick felt himself relax contentedly. The one question that had troubled him—the reaction of his father and all Bannaventa to his piety and his consciousness of God—had been answered in the most satisfactory way. "It is a wonderful gift," he finished.

Decurion Calpornius nodded. "The fear remained in us

until none of us would forget it. Then God gave us a new gift when He allowed that King Neal to die. We had no more trouble from the Irish after that."

Patrick thought of his own life when the King had been killed. He laughed as he remembered all that Erc had told him. "The new king was busy trying to get the throne and has been too busy holding it—he couldn't risk a raid against Britain."

Knowledge of the change in his father and the people of Bannaventa removed the last obstacle to the happiness Patrick had anticipated in the achievement of his goal. In the days and weeks that followed, his happiness grew and strengthened in the recognition of familiar surroundings— the villa, the garden through which he had charged on the night he had been taken captive, the fields where men and women worked placidly, the forest beyond the village, a wild flower-filled bush that marked the turn in the road, the place beside the river where he and other boys of the village had first learned to throw spears and competed against each other until he won so consistently that the contests had ended.

Yet happiness did not immediately bring the peace he had expected. He was restless from an inner excitement that drove him each day to see the workers in the field, the people in the village, the small hiberna his father had commanded, deserted now and falling into ruin. He knew his restlessness—knew his physical need for moving about and exhausting the energy that was accumulating within him instead of being dispelled by the tensions of life as it had been during his ten years of slavery and wandering.

His father and Bannaventa watched understandingly. They had seen other youths return after their years of service in the Legion; they knew the restlessness that followed the abrupt change from active military life to the placid and normal civilian life; they knew that the restlessness must be much greater in one who had lived an even more harrowing existence. They marked those periods when his restlessness increased, and they exerted themselves to calm his spirit. "They urged," he wrote, "that, after suffering so many hardships, I must not again depart but should remain and enjoy life with them."

Rapprochement between his father and himself advanced swiftly, the more so because they were to each other as men of equal stature rather than father and son. It was as to a friend that Patrick disclosed the continuing restlessness within him.

Decurion Calpornius knew only one remedy for the restlessness of man. "Find a wife, son," he counselled. He spread his arms wide to indicate the villa and surrounding fields. "There isn't a young woman in the district who would refuse this."

Patrick smiled amusedly. "She should marry me, not this villa."

His father shifted his great frame impatiently. "There isn't a woman in Britain who would refuse a man of your size and manner," he retorted, assuming again the pride of earlier days.

Patrick accepted the comment without interest. Those who had been the companions of his youth were all married—mothers and fathers as proud of their children as his father was of him. He had visited their homes and seen their evident contentment; he was aware of the interested but covert glances of their younger sisters. For a time he wondered at his disinterest; then he began to assume direction of villa and fields, relieving his father of the burden and finding increasing peace.

Slowly the consciousness of well-being effaced the memory of past deprivations; his unimpeded freedom to walk wherever and whenever he willed countered the memory of those years when he could move only when permitted and directed by another. With the treasure remaining from Senator Pinianus' gift, he added lands, purchased cattle and pigs and, to the surprise of those who knew of his years as a slave-shepherd in Ireland, sheep. He brought a new and undreamed prosperity to the villa by the energy of his work and direction until the names of Decurion Calpornius and his son, Patrick, were known well beyond the district of Bannaventa.

There were periods of intense thoughtfulness—periods when his very success, or a chance word of his father, or an incident reminiscent of the past, made him reappraise his pleasure and contentment. He made them periods when he reminded himself that he enjoyed whatever he enjoyed because of God's bounty; he wondered anew at the evidence of God's liberality.

He was sensitive to the leisure he enjoyed; deliberately he reminded himself of the time when Senator Pinianus had spoken of leisure, its uses and abuses—"time that may be given to religion, study, relaxation and other good activities but which the majority waste away in idleness or the excessive pursuit of pleasure." He had neither means nor cause nor even desire for the study of worldly things other than those relating to the villa and fields; but he had ample time and a compelling desire for that greater study which is a part of religion.

More and more deeply he impressed upon himself

the consciousness of God; more and more profoundly, he received a knowledge of God. As his material well-being improved and his wealth increased during the fourteen untroubled years from 411 to 425, Patrick multiplied his spiritual wealth.

They were years in which "God made me fit," as Patrick commented; they were also years in which Patrick, his mind relieved of distracting cares and strains, centered his thoughts and desires upon Almighty God.

*   *   *   *   *

The untroubled years ended in a series of disappointments and reverses. Decurion Calpornius died in the early summer of 425, the village pastor a month later. An unseasonal snow and frigid air swept down from the north in August, destroying field crops and fruits. In September, the resurgent Irish raced in from the sea to take captives from the villages along the coast and strike terror into all of Britain.

Patrick was forty, an age ill suited to solitary life in a villa where each room, each bench, each inanimate thing within the house and the animate things outside all reminded him of the man who was not only his father but his friend. The house itself seemed suddenly to have expanded with the removal of his father's massive bulk. Patrick was lonely.

Death of the village pastor, the loss caused by the fury of the elements, and the raid by the Irish were of less significance to Patrick at the time. Loss of the pastor was spiritual rather than personal, loss of the crops an inconvenience, the raid by the Irish a distant threat. Years later, he would realize that all three served God's purpose: Loss of the crops reminded him forcefully of man's dependence on

God's providence; the raid by the Irish—soon followed by others—made those barbaric people the foremost topic of conversation among all Britons; and loss of the village pastor brought Father Deisignatus to replace him.

In many ways, the new priest was the direct antithesis of the old. He was young—fifteen years younger than Patrick; he was learned in the wisdom he had received in a monastery at Auxerre in France, learned in worldly wisdom derived from the reading of many ancient manuscripts. He brought a great confidence in his ability and an eagerness to apply his learning, both worldly and spiritual, to life in Bannaventa; he had an ebullient good humor to mollify those who resented his energetic guidance of their lives.

Patrick's loneliness and the priest's weakness for a life more comfortable than he had endured at Auxerre brought the two men together. The priest had found a patron with whom he could enjoy the small pleasures of life without censure or condemnation; Patrick had found a friend to relieve the void of his lonely life.

"You should find a wife, Patrick," Father Deisignatus suggested almost immediately. "It is not good for man to be alone—I quote the prophet," he added with a grin.

Patrick smiled amusedly at the younger man's confident assurance in his solutions to all of life's problems. "You and my father would have been great friends; he prescribed the same remedy."

In later months, though other subjects often claimed their attention and conversation, the young priest returned tenaciously to his recommendation that Patrick deliberately seek a wife. For a time, Patrick evaded both agreement and disagreement by parrying the younger man's recommendations, but as their friendship increased and the other's insistence grew correspondingly, the spirit of friendship demanded an explanation of him.

They were together in the villa on a wet, foggy day, late in December of 425, when Patrick told fully of his father's recommendation and his own study of the matter. "I am much older now than I was then—more than twice as old as girls of marriageable age. I would be marrying a child of my youthful companions."

"There are widows," Father Deisignatus objected.

Patrick refrained from the answer he had earlier determined upon to that suggestion. Indeed there were widows, more now than fourteen years ago, but the few who indicated interest in marrying again invariably betrayed a spirit of acquisitiveness for the villa rather than interest in him.

And there was some other influence within him, he knew—an influence he could not define but which he knew was most surely present. His deliberate and conclusive rejection of marriage had effected some change within him as radical and fundamental, though completely contrary to, the change produced in other men by marriage.

"It may be," he continued after a time, "that God forced me to live so closely to Him through those years in Ireland and Rome that the ordinary attractions of life have lost their power over me."

"Nonsense," the priest answered bluntly. "You experienced nothing more than other men did; the only difference between you and them is that you escaped and have been able to live again as a free man. If those others had escaped, do you think they would speak of 'knowing' God or 'living close' to Him?"

Patrick realized that he was being driven either to some untenable position or into one which he could justify only by revealing more of the days in Ireland than he had ever revealed to others. He attempted to evade Father Deisignatus' urgings, but the other would not permit escape by that device. Finally Patrick realized that he even welcomed the opportunity of telling about the voice that had spoken to him.

"There is one difference between me and the others who were in Ireland," he began. He proceeded to tell of the multiplicity of events that had preceded actual escape from Ireland, of the voice that had spoken to him twice, of the journey across France with Aelred and the other two Irish, and of the voice that returned to scold him.

The priest's habitual expression of light humor vanished as he listened to the account of the mysterious voice that had spoken on three occasions. He did not doubt; he was astonished, then awed, by Patrick's account. "That was the voice of God!" he exclaimed. "And He spoke to you—a layman?" He paused and studied Patrick intently. "Patrick, I retract my advice to you that you marry. You should be a priest—no, you should be a bishop," he finished triumphantly.

Patrick smiled at his friend's ready enthusiasm. "I'll be content if God will permit me to remain a freeman so that the voice will never again be necessary to tell me when to escape." He frowned slightly as he recalled the other occasion on which the voice had spoken to him. "And I'll pray that I may never again do—or fail to do—something for which God must punish me."

Father Deisignatus would not be persuaded against his new advice. "You are already failing," he insisted, "by your refusal to do what you should. Patrick, that voice need not return in order to inform you that you should be a priest, then bishop. You are supposed to use your own intelligence to understand that."

Patrick shook his head in disagreement. "I've thought of the priesthood," he admitted. "But . . ."

"Not just the priesthood," the priest interrupted heatedly. "Patrick, any man to whom God speaks is destined to a bishopric."

"Not a man who once defied God," Patrick answered firmly. "I was not worthy of God's favor. Before I was humiliated, I was like a stone immersed in the slime of the earth. There was a day—I do not know if I was then fifteen—there was a day when the priest who taught us in the school told me that I should go to hell if I continued my attitude of that time. I achieved such a summit of defiance against him that day that I answered, 'If there is such a place as hell, let God now strike me dead and send me there.'"

The priest waved his hand impatiently. "That was merely the rebelliousness of childhood. God gave you a great grace long after He punished you for that." He straightened resolutely. "Patrick, I will go to the bishop myself and tell him what you have told me. I will sponsor your vocation to the priesthood." His light humor returned as he arrived at his decision. "I will be sponsoring you as bishop, too, but the bishop of Deva will not know that."

Patrick moved his head slowly to refuse. "If God wished me to be a priest, He would have given me some inner inclination. I have none. I am content with what He has given me."

"I am the better judge of that," the priest said sharply.

Carefully Patrick let some moments pass without speaking. He knew and understood that youthful assurance which deceived the priest and led him now to recommend what he should not. He remembered the self assurance he himself had once suffered; and remembered, too, the sudden anger that had followed when any presumed to challenge his opinions and decisions. He did not wish Father Deisignatus to descend to that step. "We will talk of this another time," he offered.

*   *   *   *   *

Patrick was not required to discuss the matter again with Father Deisignatus. Immediately after their conversation, the Irish struck again on the western coast, farther to the north than had been their custom; but, contrary to other occasions, a determined band of Britons assembled quickly from the villages of the district, killed a third of the raiders and drove the remainder back to their boats.

All Britain rejoiced in the unexpected victory; all hailed a man, Coroticus, once decurion of the Legion, who had organized the villagers of his district and led them to victory.

Father Deisignatus forgot completely the matter of Patrick's "destined" future as priest and bishop. He enthused, with his usual extravagance, about the victory in the north and the man who was responsible for it. He found a reason for reporting to the bishop at Deva—not to mention Patrick—but to learn more about the leader of the Britons; be returned to Bannaventa to sing the praises of Coroticus without restraint.

Patrick welcomed the subject that had distracted the priest from continuing the discussion of his own life. He let the young priest talk uninterruptedly and, when occasion required, offered comments designed to encourage him.

Another raid by the Irish and another victory by the villagers commanded by Coroticus impelled Father Deisignatus to hurry again to Deva. When he returned to Bannaventa, he glowed with a new admiration for Coroticus. "This time," he disclosed to Patrick, "he allowed only a few of the Irish to escape so they could return to their own and tell them that the rest who were not killed have been enslaved. That will discourage them from continuing these raids," he enthused.

A tremor shook Patrick. In a single moment, all the dread memories he had struggled to suppress and forget emerged from the deep recesses where they had lain hidden for so many years. He did not want to be reminded of slavery, even by enslavement of the barbaric Irish. He resented the animated glibness with which this young priest recounted the utility of slavery as a deterrent against other raids by the Irish. He spoke slowly, deliberately avoiding all indication of impatience with the other. "Rome has been discouraging slavery."

Father Deisignatus regarded him indignantly. "This is not Rome, Patrick. Rome abandoned us to those barbarians twenty—twenty-five years ago when they withdrew the last legion. What Rome discourages does not affect us."

Patrick shook his head patiently. "I did not mean the Roman government; I referred to the Roman Church."

The priest flushed with annoyance, but he retained his habitual good humor. "I am the priest for this village, Patrick," he answered patronizingly. "Rome has not had to endure raids by these Irish as we have here in Britain."

The words and the tone in which they were uttered silenced Patrick. He could not speak lest he speak angrily against Coroticus or any other—even this young priest—who would contribute to revival of slavery for any reason. The long years of self-discipline asserted themselves. He knew the futility of reminding this young man—a priest but yet a young man—of that time when the Goths had surged into Rome. Father Deisignatus had been a boy of ten in far-off Britain at the time; the tragedy of Rome's death and the greater event of the emergence of the Church's independence were not of significance to him.

He was glad to abandon the subject. The mere discussion of it reopened the scars traced across his back by the lash, chilled him as had the snow and rain when he followed Master Miliucc's sheep, brought a wave of weakness as he remembered the hopelessness of the years when he had endured in prayer.

In that instant, he was conscious that he wished to be rid of the young priest, not alone because of the issue between them, but because he had seen briefly into the heart of the other and did not want to continue the sight. They were not and never had been true friends, he realized. The other had sought his company for reasons of self-interest rather than because of mutual interests on which true friendship is founded; and he had tolerated the younger man's undisciplined enthusiasms, self-gratification and self-confidence as weaknesses of youth. He could not tolerate the disobedience which the other now revealed. He let his silence bring their meeting to an end.

During the days and weeks that followed, Patrick was away from the villa for long periods and more often than had been his custom. Servants informed him of visits by Father Deisignatus, but when he did encounter the priest, he neither explained his absences nor expressed regret for them. It was his only defense against painful memories of the past which he sought to forget.

He was not permitted to forget. New bands of Irish swept in from the sea to raid the western coast, seize prisoners, and return to their homeland. One group landed in the north, in the section dominated by Coroticus, and were themselves captured and enslaved; in the wake of that victory, the former decurion extended his authority over other districts along the western coast and his influence deep into the interior.

Dreams disturbed Patrick at night as memories tormented the days. He awakened one night while plunging from his couch and knew he had dreamed of another night when he had lunged forward in an attempt to help a weak girl. He sat shivering on the edge of the couch as he remembered the knife that had glinted briefly in the light of the fire.

The dreams were without sequence. On another night he heard the barking of dogs and thought that he raced across the snow-covered earth to lunge with the sharpened point of his crook against a great beast. He felt again the stinging blow as the bear pawed at him.

On a night in the early summer of 426, Patrick dreamed of the star-filled night when he had tried to encourage Victoricus to continue their flight. Again he experienced the same struggle within himself of refusing to recognize his friend's weakness. "If we rest a few days," he repeated the words of that night.

Word by word, minute by minute, he relived that night until Victoricus whispered hoarsely, "Keep the Faith," and slumped lifeless. He leaped up, as he had that night, and the effort awakened him. He sat on the side of the couch looking at the things in the room, lighted by the night candle—the things that symbolized his freedom and contentment. Much of the night fled by before he was able to lie back on the couch.

"Then I saw in the night the vision of a man whose name was Victoricus coming to me from Ireland, bearing countless letters. He gave me one of them and I read the opening words, 'The voice of the Irish.' Even as I read, I heard their voices." Twenty years became as one. He heard again the hated language—the language he had learned only that he and Victoricus might escape—the language he had struggled to forget. He had learned well; he had not forgotten it. He understood the voices speaking to him.

"The voices were of those who lived beside the Wood of Voclut, which is near the western sea. And they cried out to me as with one voice, 'We beg you, come and walk with us once more.'"

He knew the voices even though all sounded together as one. There was Dichu's and Eilethe's and her sister's. There was Erc's. Strangely, there were also the voices of Aelred and his young partners, the three who had fallen beneath the knives of the Suevi. He knew each voice and yet knew also the one voice into which all were combined. It was the soft, rich voice that was the voice of God or of God's angel.

He knew also the message they spoke to him—"come and walk with us once more." They asked him to walk with them only once, but that once must be for the remainder of his life. "I was brokenhearted. I could read no more of the letters. And I awakened."

He sat up again, arousing himself completely to the comfort of the room, the pleasantness of this life he knew. It was a mere dream, he told himself—a dream like the others, incited by the news of the Irish raids in the west. It was a dream, a dream, he insisted; it was not a vision but a mere dream.

The voice? It had not been the voice of God or God's angel. Sleep had deceived him. It was a blending of Dichu's voice and Eilethe's, or Erc's and Aelred's, so that it was soft and rich. But it could not have been the voice of God or God's angel because he would not permit it to be.

He would not go to Ireland, he resolved. The voice that had guided him—the voice that had first alerted him, then had told him that his ship was ready, would not now tell him to return to the very place from which he had barely escaped with his life. Having delivered him from mortal danger, it would not now place him in jeopardy; having delivered him from slavery, it would not now tell him to return to slavery.

He thought of lying down, but he knew he would not sleep; he would merely lie awake, dreading to sleep lest the dream return. He stood up and went through the double doors into the garden, sweet with the scent of the summer night.

During the nights that followed, he slept fitfully and awakened early, always before dawn. By day, he walked about restlessly, going far from the villa as though distance and physical exhaustion would eradicate the illusion from his mind.

He had suffered an illusion, he determined. It was an illusion because the realities of life were the villa and surrounding fields, the village and his friends, his liberty— the contrary realities were those barbarians, the Irish, and enslavement. The reality was Coroticus and the others who countered slavery with slavery. These were realities;

the experience of the night was an illusion or a dream or a deceit of the devil.

The memory of Aelred and his companions haunted him—the three who had died without knowledge of God or faith in Christ. Others of the Irish would die—Dichu and Eilethe and Erc—equally ignorant of God and the Savior unless he . . .

He would not! He would not succumb to the folly of believing a mere dream.

He tried to forget Victoricus and, the more he tried, so much the more clearly did he hear the Roman's lament, "There were times when I thought God might let me escape so that I could return home, study, receive Holy Orders and return to these people." It was that memory, he decided, that had made him see Victoricus again and had made him see those letters and hear the voice.

Gradually he persuaded himself. Through the remaining weeks and months of 426, he exerted himself until at last he knew he had won the victory. At long last, he was able to relax quietly at night, to eat fully, to attend the affairs of the villa, without striding off suddenly on purposeless journeys. He grew calm again.

"And, on another night—whether within me or not—they called me most unmistakably with words which I heard but could not understand." The voices came faintly as from a great distance—or a great depth.

He struggled from his couch as he had months earlier to look vacantly at the candle flickering on the table and the shadows that formed and fled as live things about the room. A dream! A dream! He was more certain now. The voices were not as they had been before, clear and distinct. They were faint and muffled.

The flame of the candle rose and fell, lifting high, then dropping down quickly. It acted in the manner of all flames whether of earth or purgatory or hell. But this was tiny and noiseless—the quiet light of a servant—while those other flames would roar frighteningly, whipping about as with a great wind, smothering the pitiful cries of those immersed within their depths.

He felt the coldness of the room, but felt also the sweat start from his forehead and over all of his body. The voices had been faint and muffled—and the flames of purgatory and hell were those that could smother the pitiful cries of souls tormented. "Almighty God! You can't design that I return?" He bowed his head and supported it with his hands. He prayed—prayed as Christ once had prayed in an agony of torment.

At times he slept; at other times he was awake; yet he seemed to continue his prayer without interruption. Occasionally he looked at the candle, measured the small amount that had burned. The night seemed endless. "They called me most unmistakably with words which I heard but could not understand"—voices that were faint and muffled as though smothered and distorted by great leaping flames. Patrick felt his very soul writhing with agony and he could pray no more.

Another voice sounded in the night. "He that has laid down His life for thee—He it is Who speaketh in thee." Patrick groaned.

"And I saw Him praying, as it were, within my body; and I heard Him pray above me, that is, over my very soul; and He prayed mightily with many groanings. And all the time I was astonished and fearful, and wondered within myself who could pray within me. But at the end of His prayer He spoke and said that He was the Spirit. And so I awoke full of joy."

His elation of the moment effectively obscured the difficulties, the certain dangers, the privations inseparable from the mission. In that elation, he discerned a new significance in the series of events that had marked the years since his return to Britain: the death of his father, loss of the crops, and estrangement from Father Deisignatus which re-emphasized the transitoriness of earthly things and affections; the raids by the Irish and the countermeasures devised by Coroticus which had revived interest in that ancient conflict and claimed his attention.

He felt a new strength—not to contemplate the hideous realities or possibilities of the ordeal before him, but to consider the immediate measures. He would sell the villa. He would go to Auxerre in France, to the monastery where Father Deisignatus had studied. He would prepare himself—as he had prepared himself so long ago when he had awaited deliverance from the Irish. He would prepare himself by study and prayer while he awaited the moment when God chose to return him to Ireland.

12

THROUGH four years, from 427 to 431, Patrick labored to learn what others absorbed without effort. His age impeded the acquisition of knowledge, he knew, but he saw also a more serious defect: "It was my sins that prevented me from fixing in my mind what once I would have learned merely by reading."

His habitual tenacity sustained him during those years; he pursued his new objective with the same concentration with which he had pursued every objective. There were times when he weakened—times when the necessity of listening to lectures and absorbing them, or reading with painful slowness designated manuscripts wearied him almost past bearing. At times he faltered, discouraged by his slow progress, by an ever-present consciousness of unworthiness—"I was not worthy," he complained against himself, "nor was I such that the Lord should grant this to His servant, that He should give me so great a grace in behalf of that nation—a thing which, in my youth, had never occurred to me." There were also times when he was discouraged by the evident doubts of superiors that God would call to the priesthood a man already past forty, or when he was antagonized against his mission by the unconcealed amusement of the youths present with him at Auxerre.

The most serious discouragement came from within rather than from without. The joy he had experienced on the night when the Spirit had spoken within him smothered slowly as he thought, with increasing frequency, of the mission itself. With painful vividness, he remembered the past in Ireland: his first frantic efforts to escape, the recurrent periods when the spirit languished beneath the depressing knowledge of his enslavement, the brutality of Dann and Master Miliucc, the coarse and monotonous food, the cold, snow, and rain when he had tended the sheep.

He had no power to close his memory to the past. It had been too deeply impressed to remain concealed when every day carried him closer to the very places where he had endured that past—where the mere sight of grass and forest would reopen the long-closed scars—where he might even be subjected to the same life again.

He would not turn back! He would do that which he had been commanded to do however hateful the task itself. If God could become mere man, then a man could become a mere slave. He knew he could abandon the mission assigned to him; but he knew he could do it only by turning completely from God.

Germanus, Bishop of Auxerre, emerged as an unfailing source of strength in days of discouragement. At their first meeting, when Patrick told of the mission assigned to him and of the earlier incidents which validated its genuineness, the Bishop had listened with such a placid expression that Patrick felt driven to ask, "Do you believe me, Bishop Germanus?"

The Bishop laughed readily, not as a man of high position laughs at one more lowly, but as a man amused by a challenge to something beyond his capabilities. "Patrick, I believe with certainty only the word of God and teachings of the Church. I hope I do not offend you," he added quickly.

Patrick shook his head. He felt disappointed that the Bishop had not immediately endorsed his recital; at the same time, he was aware of an urge to confide in this prelate whose great height and obvious strength seemed incongruous with his position.

"I don't disbelieve you," Bishop Germanus continued. "Perhaps you will be more assured of that if I tell you that I was a soldier until the day before I became a priest—and just a year before I become Bishop of Auxerre." He smiled broadly at Patrick. "I was the centurion commanding the garrison here when Bishop Amator summoned me one day and told me that he would ordain me on the next. Since then, Patrick, I've never had any inclination to doubt God's ways, however strange they may seem to be."

Their friendship, begun the first day of meeting, developed and deepened. As often as Patrick wished or felt the necessity for so doing, he would trudge up the steep, narrow street to the residence of the Bishop; when Bishop Germanus wished a respite from the press of visitors, he summoned Patrick and, closeted with him, enjoyed a time of relaxation.

An order from Rome in 429, dispatching Bishop Germanus with neighboring Bishop Loup to Britain for a synod, closed off this source of comfort and strength to Patrick. For a time after departure of the Bishop, he sought a new friend among those with him in the monastery—one who could supply the strength needed in times of depression—but all, without exception, were more interested in questioning him about the Bishop's mission, of which he was ignorant, than helping him.

Couriers arrived and departed regularly during the two years that Bishop Germanus was absent, carrying information of diocesan affairs to him, bringing his instructions on their return. Of the synod, the couriers could tell only that it had issued a new and strongly worded edict against the resurgence of slavery in Britain and ordered it discontinued; the bishops had even ransomed a number of the Irish and permitted them to live in the same quarters as themselves until they could arrange to return them to their own people. Their action had inspired many of the Britons to release slaves they had purchased and send them to the bishops.

The reported interest of the bishops in the enslaved Irish aroused Patrick. He had no desire to search the reports for greater significance, but tried to find in them a reason for a more cheerful spirit within himself, tried to apply himself more diligently to study, tried to resign himself completely to his destined mission.

He knew he was failing in his effort; when Bishop Germanus returned to Auxerre in 431, after his absence of two years, Patrick admitted that the long period had drained his strength until it had approached a most dangerous level. When he was summoned by the Bishop, only two days later, he climbed the hill heavily.

In the first instant of meeting, Patrick was aware of a certain misgiving or hesitancy in the manner of the Bishop. Bishop Germanus was obviously struggling to preserve an appearance of joyfulness at his return and their meeting; but his effort failed. He seemed dejected and reluctant to progress beyond the meeting itself. Their conversation failed, and they sat facing each other, uncomfortably silent.

"Have you heard anything of the synod?" the Bishop asked, after a time.

Patrick nodded. "We learned of the edict about slavery, of the ransom paid by the bishops and the release of slaves by some Britons."

Bishop Germanus wagged his head soberly. "We disagreed violently—the synod nearly ended in the first week." He paused, apparently seeking agreeable words for expressing his thoughts. "Patrick," he resumed quietly, "I think I should forewarn you that I must tell some unpleasant and discouraging news." He waited for Patrick's nod of acknowledgment.

"The synod was convened for a number of reasons. One was this matter of enslaving other human beings, especially the Irish, and that became immediately the most important of all questions. I need not review the background of the matter—you probably know that much better than I.

"When the subject was first introduced, the bishops of Britain opposed issuance of an edict—they said that enslavement of the Irish was Britain's only means of defense against those people. They emphasized that since Britons had begun to enslave those Irish raiders they were able to capture, the Irish had first diminished, then stopped their raids entirely. They insisted that releasing the slaves and returning them to Ireland would inspire new raids.

"The rest of us, including Pope Celestine's representative, could not condone slavery as a means of self-defense—we contended that it was nothing but another form of ransom, one even more pernicious than demanding payment of gold. The bishops of Britain opposed us strongly; one of them referred to what he called a great raid of thirty years ago. Was that the raid when you were taken?"

Patrick nodded. "They call it the great raid now because of the number who were taken to Ireland and enslaved," he answered briefly. He was anxious for Bishop Germanus to disclose the news he had described as unpleasant.

"It was the remark of that one bishop that suggested a possible solution to our disagreement," the Bishop continued. "I thought of you and your mission. I proposed that, in addition to issuing an edict for the people of Britain, we must also send missionaries to Christianize the Irish. Some of them objected strongly that no man would venture among the Irish, even for the sake of Christ and human souls, but I was able to assure them that I already knew a man who would; I told them I was confident that the man could enlist others to accompany him. Then I told them of you, your time as a slave in Ireland, your knowledge of the Irish language, and your willingness to go there."

Patrick felt himself shrinking and cowering within the innermost recesses of his soul. Even the words "slave" and "Irish" were sufficient to revive the most dreadful of his memories.

"I knew," Bishop Germanus had continued, unaware of the effect of his words, "that the whole controversy was settled even before I stopped talking. One of the prelates, who had been most opposed, discovered something that had not occurred to me: He pointed out the peculiar qualifications God had given you—your physical strength both for the work and for the admiration of the Irish, the peculiar chain of events which led you to become so proficient in their tongue, and especially your love of God which incited you to return to a people who had treated you so badly. All the prelates were so completely satisfied that they approved issuance of the edict against slavery that same day.

"About a week intervened. We had proceeded to other matters when one of the bishops revived the subject of

Ireland. He said he had been informed that you had publicly denied the reality of hell."

Patrick started as though he had been struck physically. His astonishment made him stare dumbly at Bishop Germanus as a man who stumbles unexpectedly on some horrible and revolting scene. "Deisignatus!" he gasped. "Father Deisignatus!" Twice again he opened his mouth to speak but closed it again without uttering a sound. The injustice of the accusation staggered his mind; anger mounted within him. "The Bishop of Deva told you of that," he charged. "One of the priests of his diocese, Father Deisignatus, told him about it." Disgust and revulsion tinged Patrick's words and harshened his voice. In hurried, scornful words, he told of the incident of childhood and the occasion when he had divulged it to Deisignatus.

A soldier's scowl swept across Bishop Germanus' face. "That happened more than thirty years ago!" he exclaimed.

Patrick leaned back. The passion drained from him, leaving him cold and rigid. "Thirty years," he agreed. "They bring against me an incident that happened—I do not know whether I was yet fifteen years old."

Bishop Germanus lowered his head sorrowfully. "If I had only known—if I had only known," he murmured. "We had already agreed that you would go to Ireland as bishop," he continued plaintively.

Patrick felt no inner response to the Bishop's astonishing admission. His mind raged with the knowledge of the injustice against him. "I am not sure," he said evenly, "that I care any longer to go to Ireland—or even to be a priest." He stood up to leave. "I am grateful to you," he acknowledged.

Bishop Germanus raised his head, then arose quickly to grasp Patrick's arm. "Stay for a time, Patrick," he pleaded.

He pressed firmly on Patrick's arm. "You have no cause to be angry with me."

Repeatedly during the course of that day Patrick arose to leave; as often as he did Bishop Germanus prevailed on him to remain longer. Daylight was fading when Patrick arose determinedly and refused to be seated again.

Bishop Germanus studied him regretfully. "You are not the first, Patrick, to be angered by the misdeeds of a priest. Neither will you be the last."

Patrick nodded his head in vigorous agreement. "I've heard that sermon often in my forty-six years," he answered bitingly. "Priests are human," he quoted. "Priests are subject to faults. Priests sometimes fail their great office. But people are also human, Bishop Germanus. People are also subject to faults and people sometimes fail to have the humility to accept and endure the difficulties imposed on them by the faults and failings of others, especially the priests."

Bishop Germanus did not attempt to counter the tirade. He seemed to accept defeat at last. His expression firmed as though he had nothing more to lose. "Are the misdeeds of one priest sufficient to make you forget the words Christ spoke to you—or which you claim He spoke to you? Are they sufficient to make you forget how Christ groaned within you?"

The words lashed Patrick's soul, pitilessly as a scourge across the back. He wanted desperately to answer—to justify himself—but his mind could not frame the words. "On that day," he recounted in his *Confession*, "I was struck so heavily that I would have fallen for all eternity. I thought the shame and blame unbearable."

"It has been your habit to pray when you are disturbed," Bishop Germanus said. "Will you pray now—for me and for yourself?"

Patrick's eyes opened with astonishment. "For you?"

"I am a priest," Bishop Germanus reminded. "I suppose I have offended others—I may even have offended some as much as this priest offended you."

Patrick moved toward the door. "I shall do well if I am able to pray tonight for myself," he answered coldly.

*   *   *   *   *

Patrick did pray that night but with an emptiness of spirit which seemed almost to negate his efforts. As often as he began, so often did there return the same thought to his mind: Why did he fail me before all the synod in a matter which once he had favored spontaneously and enthusiastically? Many hours after the others slept, he abandoned even the attempt to pray. Prayer could not flow from his injured mind and heart.

"I saw a vision in the night." Whether he were asleep or awake he did not know. "I saw a vision in the night. There was a writing without honor against my face. At the same time I heard God's voice saying to me, "We have seen the deed of Deisignatus to his dishonor and punishment."

Patrick awakened fully and lay staring into the darkness. "There was a writing without honor against my face"—the charge that, for no better cause than self-love, he had abandoned Him whom he should love above self and all else; the charge that, because of injury to his self-esteem, he was turning from Him who had suffered the most terrible injuries and death—even death on the Cross—for him.

"We have seen the deed of Deisignatus." It was as though God had repeated His words of the long-distant past, "Vengeance is mine"—especially vengeance against those who were His own ministers. It were as though God reminded him that no man may rise up against God's ministers and, for that very reason, those ministers who proved unworthy would endure so much greater punishment. It were as though God reminded him that none has a right to study the faults of others but rather should he look to his own faults—leaving the faults of others, and their punishment, to Him.

Unexplainably, he remembered the afternoon in Rome when he and Senator Pinianus walked together from the headquarters of the Twentieth Legion along the road leading to the Viminal. "We speak too glibly," his patron had said, "when we speak of faith as a gift—something given to us by God without effort on our part. It is a gift—a great gift—but none of us receives it in its fullness until God tries us and tempers us and tests our faith. Our friend, Bishop Augustine, inferred something of the sort—'He Who made you without your help will not save you without your will.' You've seen how the smiths temper metal—from the fire into the water, back into the fire and again into the water. So also does God temper our faith."

"God spared me graciously for His name," Patrick wrote of that trial, "and helped me in my affliction. Therefore, I give thanks to Him who strengthened me and did not frustrate the journey upon which I had determined. I give unwearied thanks to Him who kept me faithful in the day of my temptation. More, I am sorry for my dearest friend; I ask God that it not be reckoned to him as sin."

He never forgot that night. Years later, confronted with some who urged gifts upon him, he sensed that the gifts would scandalize others. In his *Confession* he could recount, "Many gifts were offered to me with tears and pleadings, and I offended the donors, even against the wishes of those with me; but, guided by God, I would not agree nor acquiesce in any way. As regards the heathen among whom I live, I have been faithful to them, and so I shall be. God knows that I have overreached none of them—nor thought of doing so—for the sake of God and His Church, for fear of raising persecution against them and all of us, and for fear that, through me, the name of the Lord be blasphemed.

"For, although I be rude in all things, I have tried diligently to keep myself safe for my Christian brethren and the virgins of Christ, and especially for those pious women who offered the gifts and were offended that I refused them. I did it for the hope of lasting success—that none might accuse me or my ministry of dishonesty; and that I would not give the infidels an opportunity to defame or revile even in the slightest matters.

"On the contrary, I spent money that all might receive me. I went everywhere in many dangers, even to the farthest districts beyond which no one lived, and where none had ever come to baptize, to ordain clergy, or to confirm the people. With the grace of God, I did everything lovingly and gladly for your salvation. And all the while I would give presents to the lords in addition to the fees they levied against me."

The night of crisis passed. Dawn brought a new resignation, even a slight determination. He saw himself as bound, helplessly bound by God, in bonds from which he could win release either by rebellion or by God's own action in releasing him. In the morning, he went again to Bishop Germanus to tell of the incident of the night.

Bishop Germanus listened wonderingly to the recitation. "If ever I doubted all the other incidents you told me,

Patrick, I would never doubt any of them again. Only the grace of Almighty God would have caused such a change as this."

Patrick took his place on a bench facing the Bishop. "The truth is that I don't want to go to Ireland," he admitted. "I suppose I wanted to use that fault of Father Deisignatus as an excuse for abandoning the mission. I've tried—God knows that I've tried to develop the desire of going because I was told to go." In his *Confession* he wrote bluntly, "I did not want to go to Ireland and did not go until I had nearly perished."

Bishop Germanus studied him sympathetically. "The lesson of Christ?" he asked gently.

Patrick moved his head despairingly. "I've remained hours before His image on the crucifix—I still have no desire to go."

"What of His desires? He didn't desire to hang on the cross."

Patrick raised his head slowly. "But He loved—that was the difference. He loved those who would be saved by His death—and He would do anything and suffer anything for men because He loved men. I can't feel any love for the Irish."

"You will—if you do what He has told you to do," Bishop Germanus said confidently. "He promised Him-self—as a matter of fact, He made obedience the very cause of love when He told the apostles on the night before He died to do what He had commanded so that they might love one another."

"When will I love the Irish?" Patrick challenged.

Bishop Germanus hesitated. He did not want to plunge Patrick into a new period of melancholy and despair. "Our

Lord Himself is the only one who could answer that. He was the one who made the promise." He leaned forward suddenly, inspired by a new thought. "In any event, Patrick, you need not go now or at any time in the near future."

Patrick looked questioningly at the Bishop, hopeful of the relief promised by his tone.

"I neglected to tell you last night that after . . . to tell you that the synod held to the basic agreement of sending missionaries to Ireland while forbidding revival of slavery in Britain. They prevailed on Bishop Palladius, the representative of Pope Celestine, to ask that the Holy Father send him to Ireland."

"Bishop Palladius agreed?" Patrick asked. The knowledge of his own cowardice—his reluctance to begin what he was assigned to do—rose up within him. The Bishop's nod emphasized his guilt. While he had contemplated this future with such pain, God had sent another in his stead. "Does he know their language?" he forced himself to ask.

"A few words—as many as most of us know."

Patrick's shame increased. While he cowered timidly in the safety of Auxerre, tormenting himself with visions of dreadful possibilities, a Roman bishop who lacked even knowledge of the Irish language had agreed to undertake the mission. "God is rebuking my want of courage."

Bishop Germanus grumbled impatiently. "Patrick, stop accusing yourself! If you lack courage or the desire to go to Ireland, it is because God chooses to withhold it from you."

"I never lacked courage to do whatever I wished to do."

"You would do well to remember that," the Bishop answered sharply. "It would impress on you that none of us can do God's will of ourselves—of our own strength. We can do what we desire with nothing more than natural courage—but to do what God desires requires a gift from Him." He drew a deep breath and expelled it noisily to release the tension of his own vehemence. "If and when God wants you to act, He will give you the courage necessary. Until He does, content yourself with prayer so that you will be preparing yourself as much as lies within your capabilities."

*   *   *   *   *

During the remainder of that year, Patrick prayed as Bishop Germanus had counseled; but the crisis of the night had exposed his weakness to him, and he prayed no longer for the desire but only for the courage to go to Ireland. Courage was the more necessary of the two; for a man of courage can do what is required of him without desire, but a man who desires is powerless to act without courage.

In the early months of 432, news filtered steadily across the sea and across France to Auxerre. "Ireland's king refused to hear the bishop sent to that barbaric island." "Pagan priests insulted the representative of Christ." "Irish people deliberately turned their backs to the prelate sent from Rome."

Patrick and Bishop Germanus found little material for discussion in the depressing reports. Both understood that the mission was failing; they anticipated the inevitable end; they knew that this effort would make another the more difficult.

In those months, Patrick felt the Bishop observing him—studying his expressions and actions as though striving to discover the interior man from his exterior indications. He felt a reluctance to speak assuredly of what he felt quite certain was occurring within him. It was April before he revealed, "God has given me the courage I lacked."

A smile of satisfaction appeared slowly on the Bishop's face. "Are you ready?"

Patrick regarded the Bishop with a puzzled expression. "God has given me the courage but not a desire to go. Should I go?"

The Bishop's smile faded gradually. He shook his head. "Christ had the courage," he murmured reflectively, "but He never desired that men would crucify Him. He provoked them as little as He could. Sometimes He hid Himself, sometimes He went to distant places to escape from them when they raged against Him. Once, He refused to accompany His followers into Jerusalem so that He would not arouse the anger of men. He waited, trying to soothe men, until the time came when men were required to accept or reject Him. When that time arrived, He entered Jerusalem in a great, triumphal procession."

Patrick became increasingly uncomfortable as the Bishop continued what seemed a comparison of his mission with the mission of the Savior Himself. He wanted to distract the other but could only sit, morose and silent. He was relieved when the Bishop concluded, "I suggest you wait a little longer, Patrick."

Patrick's expectations mounted in the month that followed. He felt no beginning of desire within himself—he had abandoned the very possibility that he would ever experience the desire—but he knew a rapid strengthening of determination. In mid-May, when a summons from the Bishop drew him again to the prelate's residence, he knew the day had arrived when he should volunteer to assist the Roman bishop in Ireland.

At the entrance to the Bishop's apartment, he stopped abruptly, surprised by the presence of three younger men— one of them a man of gigantic size and strength—dressed in garments that identified them as Irish. Bishop Germanus beckoned for him to enter. Unconsciously he assumed the grave expression customary to the Irish and bowed slightly to the three strangers. "To failte romhat." He moved his accustomed bench so that he would face both the prelate and the visitors. "From Bishop Palladius?" he asked the Bishop.

The prelate nodded without pleasure. "With this long letter." He indicated several pages lying on a table beside him. "Without this letter, I wouldn't have known who they are or where they are from—I couldn't understand anything they said. The sense of the letter is that the King of Ireland expelled Bishop Palladius with these three who seem to be the total of all the Irish who accepted Christianity. They went from Ireland to Britain. The Bishop remained there but the Britons, incited by Coroticus, became so indignant about the Irish expelling a bishop that they threatened these men also. The Bishop sent them here."

Patrick glanced at the three Irish. He had wondered vaguely and infrequently what his reaction would be to these people when he met them again. He knew the answer clearly now. "The people here will welcome you because you and they are Christians," he assured them in their own tongue. He stood up and approached them; the three also arose, eager to be friends with the one stranger who was not a stranger because he spoke their language as well as they did. He extended his hand to the giant, a man three inches taller and much wider and more powerful than himself. "I am Patrick," he said.

The big man seemed strangely uneasy. "I am Mantan, a servant, Master Patrick," he said quickly as though expecting Patrick to withdraw his hand. "I am a charioteer and a hunter." When he could delay no longer, he grasped Patrick's hand but released it quickly. He was not accustomed to friendliness by those he regarded as his superiors.

"Lugnaedon, Master Patrick," the next man introduced himself. He was slender and wiry. His blue eyes were unusually faded in one so young. "I am a fisherman," he added. He seemed less abashed than Mantan but only because he was encouraged by Patrick's manner toward the big man and himself.

"Keenan," the third youth said simply, without addressing Patrick as "Master" or displaying the servile manner of his companions. He stood very erect and completely at ease.

"Master Keenan is a lord, Master Patrick," Lugnaedon interjected proudly.

Patrick looked at Keenan with new interest. Only in that instant did he realize the thoughts that had been racing through his mind from the first moment of seeing the three. Intuitively he realized that they were messengers sent to summon him—a hunter to provide for them on land, a fisherman to convey them over the water, and this noble youth. . . . The youth could be a priest—the first native priest of his homeland—if he were willing to forget that he was now a lord of Ireland. "Did you know Master Miliucc, the lord of Slemish in the north of your country?"

Keenan shook his head. "My home is near Tara, the house of the king," he explained. "Are you the one to whom Bishop Palladius sent us?"

Patrick looked around to Bishop Germanus and interpreted the youth's question.

The prelate gestured toward the letter beside him. "Bishop Palladius referred to you. He said also that the bishops of Britain have decided to abandon all further effort among the Irish. I may do as I wish without consulting them."

Patrick turned again to Keenan. "I am the one."

"How do you know our language?"

Patrick saw immediately the opportunity given him. "I was a lord in Britain," he answered lightly so that his words would impress the other without offending him. "I was taken captive by King Neal's raiders, sold as a slave to Master Miliucc and served him for six years." He was satisfied with the expression of discomfort his words produced. He glanced at the other two so as to include them in his question. "Are all of you ready to return?"

The question startled Keenan more than the other two. "That's impossible," he exclaimed.

Patrick moved his head immediately in disagreement. "Nothing is impossible with God."

Keenan accepted the correction without opposition. "But we have only just been expelled. It will be very difficult to return so soon."

"That's the very reason why we should go immediately. Your people are courageous, Keenan. If we go immediately, they will recognize the courage God gives us."

He turned again to Bishop Germanus, who had listened patiently to the conversation he could not understand. "The time has come, Bishop Germanus."

13

"WE are passing my home village, Bishop Patrick."
Patrick looked up at Lugnaedon from his place in
the bottom of the boat. Reluctantly he shrugged aside the
heavy robe in which he huddled and stood up. The cold
November wind flailed at him as he raised above the level
of the boat, chilling him; he would have liked to drop down
again quickly to his place, but Lugnaedon needed someone
to look with him at the cluster of buildings on the beach,
and neither Mantan nor Keenan arose.

"He is homesick, Bishop Patrick," Mantan taunted from
his shelter in the bow. His great length stretched nearly to
the mast that creaked in its socket as it responded to the pull
of the sail. "Don't pity him, Bishop Patrick—he laughed at
me when I was seasick."

Patrick had grown accustomed to the bantering of the
two that served both to unite them and to separate them
from himself and Keenan. "Can we put in here?"

Lugnaedon looked longingly at the village but shook
his head. "When they saw me, they would treat us worse
than the others did." Abruptly, as though some crisis had
occurred, he drew in the oar that served also as tiller. "Mantan, drop the sail. It is time to come about."

Patrick dropped down to his place and drew his robe
close about him. During these days when they coasted along

203

the Irish shore, he had learned to regret the years of warmth and comfort at Bannaventa and Auxerre. God, he decided, should have caused him to live at the mercy of His elements as he had in his youth; then the discomfort of life on the water would not intensify the discouragement of rejection by those on the land.

He was dejected, he admitted. He had not anticipated that they would be forbidden to land—that the Irish would thrust them back into the sea. Grim humor stirred feebly, and he looked at Keenan slumped down on the opposite side of the boat. "It was easier to escape your country than it is to enter it."

Keenan moved uncomfortably as he always did when Bishop Patrick referred to his days of slavery. "King Leary must have issued an edict against Christians," he answered apologetically. "In his mind—and the minds of the people—Christians are Romans, and the Romans in Britain planned long ago to invade Ireland."

Patrick leaned his head back against the side of the boat, watching Lugnaedon and Mantan at the complex task of changing course, raising and securing the sail. He could not dispute Keenan's analysis nor his defense of the Irish; had God left him to his own devices, he himself might have been among those who desired to invade this country by force, subdue it, then impose Christianity upon the people. His mind reverted to the days when he had lived in Rome— days when he had known that God held him there, almost as a prisoner, but without disclosing His reason. He knew the reason now: He had witnessed the death of the Roman state, he had witnessed the continuing life of the Church. Even then, God had been forming him. "If ever we land, Keenan," he said slowly, "we must impress on the Irish that we are not Irish nor Romans nor Britons. We will tell them only that we are Christians."

The younger man's expression softened as it lost some of its defensive belligerence. "Bishop Palladius tried to tell them that," he answered. "They would not believe him."

"They knew he was a Roman?"

Keenan nodded. "Roman and Christian, Christian and Roman." He looked at his superior warningly. "They will think of you as Briton and Christian, Christian and Briton."

"But I'm not a Briton," Patrick disclaimed.

"You said you were a lord . . ." Keenan reminded.

"I wasn't born in Britain, Keenan, I am . . ." He stopped suddenly. A sly smile appeared. "I was born a Christian, Keenan. I am a Christian." The slight smile faded as his attention returned to the problems of the present. "We must land before we will be able to say anything to your people, Keenan. What of your friends? Aren't there some along this coast who know you and would permit us to land?"

Keenan muttered indistinctly but indicating clearly his doubts that any would ignore an edict of the King. His original estimate of the difficulty they could expect had been amply confirmed; their repeated efforts to land had increased his pessimism. "One of my father's kinsmen, Master Nathi, is lord of a district farther up the coast," he said hesitantly. "When my father died, he sent his men to help me hold the lands my father owned. But he's one of King Leary's most trusted supporters."

"We can try him," Patrick suggested.

Keenan shrugged his shoulders. "He should be no worse than the others. But if he drives us away, we may as well return to Auxerre." He looked up at Lugnaedon and

described Master Nathi's area until Lugnaedon assured him
confidently that he remembered that part of the coast.

A steady rain during the night increased Patrick's discomfort. The robe drawn around him warded off the rain,
but the dampness penetrated his chilled flesh and prevented him from sleeping. The rain ceased with the dawn,
but the wind also failed, and the sail sagged limply as the
boat pitched and rolled with the movement of the waves.
Lugnaedon and Mantan lowered the sail, fixed the oars in
their slots and began to row with short, powerful strokes
toward the shore. When they were close in, Lugnaedon
looked searchingly along the beach, then pointed to a place
a short distance farther. "Master Nathi's," he announced
triumphantly.

Patrick saw men appear on the shore as Lugnaedon and
Mantan stroked the boat to the designated place. They did
not gather into a single group around a leader as had those
at the other points; they stood along the shore in pairs and
threes, waiting to discover whether those approaching were
friends or enemies.

Keenan leaped over the side as the boat grounded. A
grumbling sound from the men lining the beach indicated
that they recognized his Roman garments as designating an
enemy, but Keenan walked unconcernedly toward the nearest pair. "We are friends," he called.

The Irish words spoken by the man dressed as a Roman
confused the two, but one of them ordered, "Stay where
you are."

Patrick, with Mantan and Lugnaedon, joined Keenan.
"Ask them for Master Nathi," Patrick urged.

A big man with two others strode from the trees behind
the beach. His face flushed angrily as he saw the dress of

the strangers. "Get off! Get off!" He stooped down suddenly and snatched stones from the beach. "Drive them off!" he shouted.

Mantan leaped in front of Patrick, shielding him with his great body from the fusillade of stones. Keenan's voice raised in angry protest. "Master Nathi! I am your kinsman!" The stoning ceased abruptly, apparently on some signal from the Master.

Patrick stepped from behind Mantan to see Keenan hurrying to confront his kinsman who stood waiting, his hands clutching more stones. A slight sound made him turn toward Mantan; the big man was pressing his hand across his mouth, blood trickled between his fingers. Lugnaedon was already urging him toward the boat.

Patrick started forward to join Keenan, but the youth turned away from Master Nathi at the same moment and motioned that they must leave the place. "He will not have a Christian as a kinsman," he explained angrily. He seemed about to say more when he saw Mantan leaning over the side of the boat scooping sea water into his bleeding mouth. He leaped upward, drew himself into the boat, turned to assist Patrick, then sat down on the rower's seat usually occupied by Mantan and drew the boat away from the shore.

Mantan interrupted his steady splashings to glance around protestingly. "I will do that, Master Keenan."

"Take care of yourself," Keenan retorted. "And stop calling me Master," he demanded. He looked back balefully on the men lining the shore. "We are Christian equals," he muttered, "not Irish lords and servants."

A shocked silence followed for some moments after the outburst, until Lugnaedon bantered callously, "And we will call Mantan the Toothless One." His voice became a shuddering groan as Mantan drenched him with cold sea water.

Patrick had settled into his usual place. He was reaching for his robe when he realized the significance of Keenan's heated exclamation. He let the robe drop and looked wonderingly at the back of the young noble, seated in Mantan's place, pulling the oar awkwardly but willingly. He had prayed for this change; he had not expected it to come under the guise of violence—he had not expected a change as complete and powerful as this. The power! the incredible power of God when man permitted God to enter into his soul!

He tugged again at the robe, drawing it around him. Why did he permit dejection to increase? Why did he permit himself to incline toward flight from this hostile land? He had not come here of his own desire; he had come only because he had been sent—sent by the God whose power would accomplish all, if only His ambassador would rely on Him, depend on Him, have faith in Him.

He had not struggled to fulfill, as he might, the command given him by God. He had distracted himself by bewailing the lack of desire to come instead of cultivating the desire merely to obey. God would have granted the desire, had it been necessary; He would grant it even now, did He so will. But He did not so will; rather did He wish His ambassador merely to obey.

God would grant that desire in time—the desire to remain among these people. God would even grant that he would someday love these people. God had promised that, and God's promises never failed.

There was a story his father had told him long ago—of a great general who had led his legionnaires to the East. To guard against desertion of his men, but more to guard against his own weakness, the general had destroyed his fleet so that he must either conquer or die.

"We will go farther north," he said loudly to Lugnaedon that the others would also hear. They would continue northward, he determined, until far above the region surrounding the King's home at Tara. They would land at some desolate place where none would appear to thrust them immediately into the sea. They would destroy the boat so that none could force them to leave and they would be unable to flee.

They came to a proper place on the second morning—a narrow channel between towering cliffs where the sea tumbled about in wild disorder. "The Dragon's Mouth," Lugnaedon said. "I've never gone through it, but others have, and they told me of it." He motioned for Keenan to take his place on the rower's seat while he moved to the stern with an oar to guide their passage.

The boat raced between barren cliffs, carried swiftly on the tide. Skillfully, Lugnaedon swept the tiller to one side or the other, guiding the boat past great rocks where the sea piled up in foaming crests. Then the waters quieted and the boat lay motionless on a long, narrow lake. A single pull on the oars brought the boat onto the shore.

Patrick followed slowly after the others, calculating their distraction. He dropped to the beach, put his shoulder immediately against the prow of the boat and pushed it out on the surface of the lake. He spun around in time to intercept Lugnaedon's instinctive attempt to recover their boat. "We came to Ireland. We are in Ireland," he told his astonished companions. He moved toward the brush surrounding the place to draw the others after him.

A dog barked. The sound seemed far away. Other

animals joined the first—the deep, throaty barking of wolf-hounds. Mantan pushed from behind to precede the group, but Patrick grasped his sleeve and drew him back. "Dogs are my friends, Mantan. If we meet any, I will talk with them."

He led the way into a long, narrow glen as two men with a cluster of leashed wolfhounds appeared at the far-ther end. The two stopped; their dogs barked furiously and plunged impatiently against their leashes.

"We are friends," Patrick shouted. His voice echoed from the slopes, but the pair at the far end seemed not to understand. Patrick moved forward, and the other pair also advanced, until Patrick could see that they were apparently a father and son. Once more he called before he realized that the noise of the dogs prevented the two from understanding him. "Quiet!" he roared in Latin. The barking stopped. "We are friends," he called again to the two men.

A single word burst from the older of the two. "Pat-rick!" The man hurried forward.

Patrick stared incredulously at the advancing figure, then hurried to meet him. "Dichu!" he answered joyfully.

EPILOGUE

WITH few words, Bishop Patrick dismissed his work in Ireland. "It would be tedious," he wrote, "to give a detailed account of all my labors or even a part of them." His labors did not interest him; the labors were not his labors, and the achievements were not his achievements. "Who was it that roused me up, fool such as I am, from among all those who are wise and skilled in law and powerful? He it was who inspired me—me, the least of all—to serve those to whom the love of Christ carried me that I might serve them humbly and sincerely."

The stylus paused again. Should he tell the greatest of all miracles God had wrought within him? Would they believe that God could so change a man? He firmed his grip on the stylus; they must believe—the Irish must never doubt that all things are possible with God. He must tell them God's final gift to him—that he loved the Irish with a deep, all-embracing, eternal love.

"Not of myself but only by the grace of God did I come to Ireland. Only by His grace did I preach the Gospel and suffer insult and persecutions and chains. Only by His grace did I give my free birth for the benefit of others. Only by His grace am I prepared now, should I be worthy, to give even my life without hesitation and most gladly for

His name. And only by His grace do I desire to remain here until I die, if the Lord so grant me."

He stopped and examined the words critically. How better could he express his love for them?

"I call God to witness that I lie not; neither, I hope, do I write to you because of avarice nor because I look to you for favor and honor. I commend my soul to God, for Whom I am an ambassador, despite my wretchedness. Let me render unto Him for all He has done to me. I must make known the gift of God; I must spread everywhere the name of God.

"Yet, what can I do or what can I write?—I who am unable to tell my story to those versed in the art of writing in such a way as my spirit and mind desire and in such manner that the words will express my meaning?"

Laboriously Patrick persisted. His big hand clutched the stylus awkwardly. The muscles of his face contracted from the intensity of his effort, magnifying the broad, heavy bones that seemed still to retain the strength of his youth. He must tell the Irish his heart's desire: that they hold themselves constantly and faithfully toward God without diminution or distraction.

"Because there is no other God, nor ever was, nor will be, than God the Father unbegotten, without beginning, from Whom is all beginning, the Lord of the universe; and His son Jesus Christ, Who has been always with the Father, spiritually and inexplicably begotten by the Father before the beginning of time, before all beginning; and by Him are all other things made, both visible and invisible. He was made man and, defeating death, was received into heaven by the Father; and He has been given all power over whatever is in heaven or on earth or under the earth, and every tongue shall confess that Jesus Christ is Lord and God, in

Whom we believe, and Whose advent we expect soon to be, judge of the living and the dead, Who will render to every man according to his deeds; and He has poured forth the Holy Spirit upon us abundantly, the gift and pledge of immortality, Who makes those who believe and obey sons of God and joint heirs with Christ; and Him do we confess and adore, one God in the Trinity of the Holy Name."

For a long time, the stylus crawled steadily across pages of parchment. The sun mounted higher, dispelling the mists and bestowing the glory of its own radiance on the land; but Patrick concentrated on the work before him—as determined in this as in any other task he had ever attempted.

At length, he stopped and looked back critically at the writing. He had not intended to digress from denunciation of himself; yet he had digressed despite himself until he had written of God rather than of himself. He read the writing again, more slowly than before, then smiled slightly with satisfaction. It was as it should be, "for this we can give to God in return for being cleansed by Him—to exalt and praise Him before every nation that is anywhere under the heavens.

"I pray those who believe and fear God—whoever deigns to read this writing which Patrick, a sinner, unlearned, has composed in Ireland—that you will never attribute good to me, however small; but let this be your conviction, that—as is the perfect truth—it was the gift of God.

"This is my confession before I die."

TAN·BOOKS

TAN Books was founded in 1967 to preserve the spiritual, intellectual and liturgical traditions of the Catholic Church. At a critical moment in history TAN kept alive the great classics of the Faith and drew many to the Church. In 2008 TAN was acquired by Saint Benedict Press. Today TAN continues its mission to a new generation of readers.

From its earliest days TAN has published a range of booklets that teach and defend the Faith. Through partnerships with organizations, apostolates, and mission-minded individuals, well over 10 million TAN booklets have been distributed.

More recently, TAN has expanded its publishing with the launch of Catholic calendars and daily planners—as well as Bibles, fiction, and multimedia products through its sister imprints Catholic Courses (CatholicCourses.com) and Saint Benedict Press (SaintBenedictPress.com).

Today TAN publishes over 500 titles in the areas of theology, prayer, devotions, doctrine, Church history, and the lives of the saints. TAN books are published in multiple languages and found throughout the world in schools, parishes, bookstores and homes.

For a free catalog, visit us online at
TANBooks.com

Or call us toll-free at
(800) 437-5876

Spread the Faith with . . .

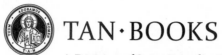

TAN·BOOKS

A Division of Saint Benedict Press, LLC

TAN books are powerful tools for evangelization. They lift the mind to God and change lives. Millions of readers have found in TAN books and booklets an effective way to teach and defend the Faith, soften hearts, and grow in prayer and holiness of life.

Throughout history the faithful have distributed Catholic literature and sacramentals to save souls. St. Francis de Sales passed out his own pamphlets to win back those who had abandoned the Faith. Countless others have distributed the Miraculous Medal to prompt conversions and inspire deeper devotion to God. Our customers use TAN books in that same spirit.

If you have been helped by this or another TAN title, share it with others. Become a TAN Missionary and share our life changing books and booklets with your family, friends and community. We'll help by providing special discounts for books and booklets purchased in quantity for purposes of evangelization. Write or call us for additional details.

TAN Books
Attn: TAN Missionaries Department
PO Box 410487
Charlotte, NC 28241

Toll-free (800) 437-5876
missionaries@TANBooks.com